AMBER SIGHTS

Behind Blue Eyes Book 4

SARA J. BERNHARDT

This book is a work of fiction. The characters, incidents, and dialogue are drawn from the author's imagination and are not to be construed as real. Any resemblance to actual events or persons, living or dead, is entirely coincidental.

First Edition

Behind Blue Eyes, book 4

2020 Lavish Publishing, LLC - Midland

Published in the United States by Lavish Publishing, LLC, Midland, TX

Cover Design by: Alexcia Productions

Cover Images: CANSTOCK

Paperback Edition

ISBN: 978-1-944985-97-4

www.LavishPublishing.com

Contents

Prologue	1
Chapter 1	5
Chapter 2	19
Chapter 3	25
Chapter 4	31
Chapter 5	41
Chapter 6	49
Chapter 7	59
Chapter 8	65
Chapter 9	75
Chapter 10	85
Chapter 11	91
Chapter 12	101
About the Author	111
Other Works by Sara J. Bernhardt	113
Also from the Lavish Family	117

For My Adam

"The best definition I can give of a vampire is a living, mischievous and murderous dead body. A living dead body! The words are idle, contradictory, incomprehensible, but so are vampires."

-John Heinrich Zopfius in his *Dissertatio de Uampiris Seruiensibus*, Halle, 1733

Prologue

HE PEERED out into the writhing darkness.

"It's bloody cold out here," he complained, rubbing his arms.

Victor smiled, not averting his eyes from the darkness ahead. He walked slowly with his hands in his pockets, distracted by almost nothing. "You don't believe me, and that's okay."

The boy smiled. "You actually expect me to believe you're a…vampire, a blood-sucking immortal, don't you?" he replied, pretending as though he couldn't possibly believe such things, though he always had.

It was then that Victor halted and stared straight into the eyes of his mortal friend. "A blood-sucking immortal?" He laughed and shook his head, continuing to walk. "Call us what you will."

"So this is what you do?" he asked Victor. "You walk along the streets at night?"

"What else is there to do?"

"Well…where do you live?"

"That depends."

"On…?"

"On what hotel I happen to stop by or what empty shed I end up in."

"What?"

"Daniel," Victor started. "It is Daniel, right?"

"Danny," the boy replied. "I like Danny."

Victor chuckled quietly. "That isn't your real name, now is it?"

He fell dumb for a moment. "How…could you know that?"

Victor lifted his arms and leaned in toward the boy with a smirk and a slight raise of the eyebrows.

The boy's brows wrinkled together in a look of confusion and disbelief. "No. No…it's…my name is William Gardner."

"Well then, Mr. Will Gardner," he started, shaking the boy's hand, "what do you say to you and me taking it back to your place, and you can listen to me continue telling you of my 'obsession' with vampires."

The boy nodded his head down once with a thin smile.

"All right then."

"Yes, I understand," he answered after a long pause, "but still if I were to tell you, would you believe me?"

He dropped his gaze, staring at his shoes. Replaying Adam's story, which Will remembered in detail, he pondered the possibilities of what was true and what was simply the fictions of a talented storyteller.

"Please tell me again, if you truly do believe it, what you

are, how you do it. How it came to be that you have this… speed, this…strength!"

"That's simple," he replied, smiling. "I've told you. I can tell you in no more than four simple words—I am a vampire." He laughed then and stared into Will's eyes. "You see? Four words and you don't believe me."

"How?" he asked quietly—thoughtfully. "How is it possible?"

"Oh, that would take so much more than four words."

"I would like to hear it," Will answered. "If…you don't mind."

He paused at first and sat back in his chair with a sigh. "I wanted you to notice these abilities I possess."

"You're serious. You're really serious." He sighed in disbelief that he was finally going to hear Victor's story, that everything he had heard from Adam was true.

"Yes," he mused. "You laugh, but perhaps my story can bring tears to your mortal eyes. You are no more than a young man who happened to notice me, and although you are nothing to me, I mean you no harm—I assure you."

He responded with a look of content and ease, sitting back in his chair with his wandering eyes, waiting for Victor to begin his tale. "So," Will started, "an evil predator of the night?"

"Contrary," Victor corrected. "Good and evil divide mortals. Such words can divide immortals as well. A life is something that most people see as temporary—they all know it will end someday. To know with certainty you will walk this earth for eternity when the times around you change but you do not, when life has no meaning anymore, when it is nothing but an unchosen, unchangeable hole of existence. When nobody, not even yourself, can understand it and to know it will never end is more terrifying and miserable than any mortal state."

"Is it painful for you to speak of this?"

"Perhaps it will be," Victor replied, "but you needn't be concerned with that."

Chapter One

IT STARTED IN 1745; I was sixteen years old and lived with my mother, my father, and two younger brothers—Charles, who was thirteen, and David, who was only ten—in Philadelphia, Pennsylvania. My father was a farmer, and we had little money. We made a living selling wheat and corn. I wished I could have helped my family with the money, but all I wanted to do was act and write poetry. My mother encouraged me. She said anything that would put bread on the table was fine by her, but my father, on the other hand, he wouldn't hear of it. He said acting and writing were for those who didn't know the meaning of hard work. I hated to work in the fields, but what could I do? Perhaps my father was right.

Sometimes, I truly felt as though I hated my father. He would never understand me. Then there was my mother, Evelyn—my sweet, beautiful mother. There was never a bitter moment between us. She had golden hair always piled upon her head and shimmering auburn eyes. She was always playing the piano while my brothers and I worked in the fields with my father, and I strained to hear those soft notes. Sometimes when I closed my eyes, I could hear her music. I would recite charming rhymes as I worked, and my father would send me inside, telling me, "You sound like a fool, and in my house, fools are not given supper."

I didn't care. It was better for him to be angry with me than be forced to stay in his company. I would go inside and listen to my mother play the piano while I recited my heartfelt poems. My mother never scolded me when I was sent inside; every time, she was happy to see me. She was always alone during the days, and she enjoyed the company.

I can clearly remember coming into her room one evening before my father was back from the fields. I saw her on her bed in her silken nightdress, combing her long, thick hair. She signaled me to come in. I sat beside her.

"Mother…" I sighed, trying to think of what exactly I wanted to say. "I want to act."

She laughed lyrically. "And wouldn't you make a lovely Romeo—or Puck, maybe."

I smiled, and she embraced me.

"I know," she whispered, "but I also know your father."

I just sighed.

"Go on to bed now. It's another long day tomorrow."

"Goodnight," I whispered as she kissed my forehead.

"Goodnight, my sweet boy."

I headed to my bedroom, trying to ignore the ache in my stomach from being denied supper again. I came into her room almost every evening after that, and as time passed, my mother grew older and older, and she didn't smile as much anymore. She had always been so beautiful, and I hated seeing the gray in her hair as she brushed it. Hated it!

Soon, I would realize how much I loved my family. At

the time, I would have been rid of my father and my brothers if I could. Charles always said just what my father did, and David would hit me. My father would have whipped me with a switch if ever I were to hit him back. I tried to be good; I tried to want to help in the fields. In the spring, I had even offered to go into town and trade some wheat and corn for an ox to help harvest the crops.

On my way, I ran into John Cornally Jr., the son of Mr. Cornally, an old friend of my father's who had moved from Georgia not but a year ago. Mr. Cornally was always trying to buy the Miller family land, but my father continuously refused, which I think really angered Mr. Cornally; he was quite a bitter man.

"Victor Miller!" John yelled pleasantly, shaking my hand.

"Hello, John," I answered, pretending as if I were happy to see him.

"What brings you into town this morning?"

"I'm here to buy an ox."

He faked a laugh. "So…has your father by any chance changed his mind about selling some of his land?"

"Not at all," I answered, turning away.

"Well, let me know if he does."

"Good day, John."

"I'm telling you. It's a good deal."

"Once again—good day, John. I need to be on my way."

He didn't press the situation this time.

"You know, I ran into John Cornally this morning," I said to my father after returning with a small ox.

He laughed, which made me smile. "Still asking about the land, I'm guessing."

"Of course. You know, Father, just selling an acre or so probably wouldn't hurt."

"No, Victor! Don't you start too. I'm a hardworking man. All of the land is growing crops, and all will be harvested. It's been wonderful for us. We have been blessed, son. Be thankful things are going so wonderfully."

"Yes," I answered softly. "I apologize."

"Yes," Charles said, "you should."

I glared at him but didn't dare respond.

It wasn't long before we ran into the Cornallys once again. I was out with my family at the market, selling the crops we had harvested. The corn was big and sweet, and the wheat was strong and unbroken. We were more fortunate than we could have ever imagined. It was a beautiful day; I couldn't take my eyes off my mother. She looked so sweet and pretty in her white flowered dress and blue apron. Lord, how I adored my mother.

"Nice day," we heard.

Of course, it was only Mr. Cornally approaching our table, wearing his strange black hat and glasses. I got a bad feeling just by looking at him. He had a very long, pointed nose and deep, desperate brown eyes that made me shiver when I looked into them.

"Yes, a very nice day," my father answered.

"I don't suppose you've changed your mind about the deal I offered you?"

"No, thank you!" he demanded desperately. "If you are going to buy something, by all means, do so, but do not continue to pressure me into selling your family my land."

"It's a good idea, Mr. Miller. It really is. You'll make a

lot more than you will trying to harvest and sell all of it on your own."

When my father denied him again, Mr. Cornally looked so angry that it frightened me a little and made my mother very nervous.

He leaned over the table and stared into my father's face. "You're a fool!" he growled. "I'll have that land—that, I can promise you." He turned away and paid us no mind the rest of the day.

John glared at me a few times as he passed by, but I just ignored.

It was a busy day. We arrived home that evening with very little left from the sale, which brought up all our spirits. We ate our fill of bread and corn, followed by my mother's rare cherry pie.

Again I was sent into town in the late afternoon, this time for our normal shopping. I hoped the Cornallys weren't there that day. They were an odd family; that I knew for sure. After I had all I was sent out for, it was beginning to get dark. By the time I had gotten home, it was past sunset.

The house was quiet. I stepped inside and gasped, dropping the bags to the floor. I felt a scream urging its way from my mouth, but I swallowed it. My hands were trembling, my body paralyzed. I could hardly move. I could feel the wetness of tears staining my cheeks. What lay in front of me was a sight that has haunted me all the days I have walked the earth. I had no conception of what had happened, only that my family was gone.

I stepped over the bleeding body of my youngest brother and into the kitchen, arming myself with a knife. I ran back to where David lay, shaking him.

"David," I demanded. "Oh God, David, please wake up!"

The tears poured from my eyes, and I began screaming.

"David! No! David, please—wake up!"

He was as limp as a rag doll; I raced through every room, confused and in utter horror. I felt cold, and my stomach was turning and twisting, bringing me to my knees in sickness. Suddenly, I came to my senses. *My God—Charles, my father…MOTHER.*

I was still on my knees. I could hardly stand. I managed to stagger to my feet, still coughing, but my vision was reddened, and I stumbled through the darkness. I realized I was holding my chest with my hands, and I trembled. Sweat flowed from every pore in my aching body. I brushed my hair from my face. The rest of the house was empty. I hoped the rest of my family had escaped. I ran out the door. I could scarcely see, but I realized I was running through the cornfields. I looked back at the house, realizing I had dropped the knife on the floor beside David. I heard soft laughter, and a grayish form emerged from the door of my house. I knew it couldn't possibly be whom I hoped, but still I yelled.

"Mother!"

More laughter. I turned my back to the house. I could see now that I hadn't run very far. I looked back once more, turned, and ran. Before I had even proceeded a few more feet, a sharp pain shot through my thigh, and I howled in agony, smashing my head upon the hard dirt. I was crying again—this time from pain. I pulled the knife from my leg and looked back at the house. I couldn't see through the corn. I couldn't see who had thrown the knife. The blood poured from the wound, and I crawled on my stomach, pulling myself with my hands, gripping the long stalk of corn, and digging my fingernails into the dirt. Darkness took my vision, and I eventually fell unconscious in the middle of the cornfield. I slept through the night, and when I awoke, it was morning.

I stood up and immediately crashed to the ground, seething in pain. I had forgotten about the wound in my leg. My eyes caught sight of a large kitchen knife in the dirt beside me. The entire blade was red with my blood all the way to the hilt. I turned away, feeling sick at the sight of it, sick to know the very bone in my thigh was exposed.

I crawled through the fields to take one last glance at my home. I peered through the green leaves, and the tears came again. I choked out a curse. The house—*my* house—was nothing but ashes.

Smoke caught in the wind billowed out from the blackened rubble, slithering into my lungs, sending me into a fit of coughs. I immediately cried out for my mother. I shouted and screamed. I even called her name—but she did not come.

I screamed until my throat was raw and I could no longer find the energy. The sobs tore from my chest. I was alone now and could think of no way I was to find help. I would surely die here in the crops, beneath the scorching sun.

I must have passed out because I awoke somewhere else. For a moment, a feeling of hope tingled in the pit of my stomach. I wasn't in the cornfields. Could it be I was dreaming? Perhaps none of it was real. A voice scattered my thoughts.

"Do not weep, young one," I heard.

I was startled for a moment. The voice echoed with a metallic ring that shot into my body. I shuddered.

"Do not weep," the voice said again.

Through my fear, confusion, and pain, I did not dare weep. I did not dare disobey. The voice was like something from a dream—a dream that made no sense but haunted me well into the morning hours.

The tears lay in my eyes, but I forced myself not to cry out, not to be afraid.

I wanted my mother and my father. I even wanted my brothers. I wanted to know they were safe, but my heart told me they were not, that they were dead now, and I was alone. My mother—the porcelain doll who received glances from all who passed her way and who people called "The fair Evelyn Miller" or "The beautiful wife of Joshua Miller"—was gone now, and my father and brothers were gone too, and I wept because I could hold it in no longer.

"Shh," I heard. "I told you not to weep."

I could feel him gently stroking my hair. I looked up and let out a cry. He was real. All real! But his skin was as white as snow and smooth—inhumanly smooth. Not a single crease, line, pore, or blemish of any kind was visible in his face. I couldn't believe he was human.

He covered my mouth with his hand. "Shh… I'm not going to hurt you. I'm only trying to help you." He removed his hand.

"Help me?"

"Yes. Don't weep now, my young beauty. I know what you want."

I shuddered again at the ring in his voice. "Revenge!" I wept. "All I want is revenge!"

He smiled, and I jumped. He had two pointed teeth on each side of his mouth, sharp like an animal perhaps—a wild beast! Then he laughed, and I started to tremble again. The laugh reverberated through the room, which I had never before seen, and I covered my ears.

"Look around now, Victor Miller, and do not ask me how I know your name."

I looked around the room and realized it looked like nothing more than an empty stable, just a little wooden room. I didn't like it. It wasn't comfortable.

"Where am I?" I asked. "Please—I want to go home!"

"It doesn't matter where you are," he said. "What matters is that you are safe now, and you will get what you seek!"

"Revenge," I whispered. "I want revenge."

"I know, and so revenge you will have if you do as I say. Listen and trust in me, and you cannot go wrong."

I smiled even though I was completely lost and miserably frightened.

"Now first, to tell you why I've chosen you."

I didn't know what he meant, but I listened.

"Amber in the eyes and sunlight in the hair." He smiled again, and his hard skin instantly softened to silk, startling me. What on earth was he? "You're beautiful, Victor, but you are hurt!"

I remembered the wound in my leg, which was still throbbing.

"Trust in me," he whispered, lifting me up.

I was sitting up now, still feeling a bit dizzy.

"I'm not going to hurt you. I'm going to save you. A wound like that will kill you, Victor—too much...*blood* loss."

No response but I was suddenly comforted by the sound of his voice.

"Trust in me," he whispered. "Trust."

I gasped when I saw his cruel, terrible teeth break into the hard skin on his wrist.

"Don't be afraid. Soon, you will feel no pain!"

He pressed his wrist to my mouth, and the blood flowed down, hot and burning, not like the blood I had tasted before but more. It was sweet yet bitter at the same time. My body craved more, but my mind knew better. This was madness; this man—was a monster!

I was gagging now and began screaming.

He covered my mouth with his hand, and his strength frightened me terribly. "Shh. Please, Victor, trust me. I am only trying to help you."

"What are you?" I whispered, still choked with fear. "What the hell are you?"

He laughed quietly. "Flesh and blood. I am flesh and blood."

No response. Blood? He tried to force me to drink *blood*! But why? Why was this? What had I done so terribly wrong that I should be punished in such a way? I must have been dreaming. This could not be real.

Wake me up, and I promise I will work hard in the fields. I promise I will obey my father. I promise I will be kind to my brothers and even to the Cornallys...

Suddenly, my thoughts froze, and every horrifying moment had replayed in my mind, intertwined with the threats and anger of Mr. Cornally. I did know—the whole time, I knew what was happening, didn't I? My body was shaking. This was *my* fault!

Oh God, please forgive me! Please forgive me, Mother, oh, my sweet Evelyn! This was my fault; I could have saved you if only I wasn't so blind. Oh God, oh God, oh God!

Who was this man here with this smile on his face? He knew something—something that he wasn't telling me.

"Yes," he said. "You see—you knew all along, didn't you?"

My rage exploded. I stood up, forgetting about the wound in my leg, forgetting that it should have hurt.

"You mock my pain!" I screamed. I began pounding him with my fists, trying to distract myself from the fact that his chest felt like a chunk of stone!

"This was your doing! You did this. You let them murder my family! I swear I'll kill you!"

I continued striking him, and in the middle of my next blow, he snatched my wrists. His speed was inhuman, and I stared at him with big, frightened eyes. I could tell by the pleasant smile he had on his hard, white face that I caused him no pain.

"I did nothing of the sort, young one," he said. "Mr. Cornally would have had your family's land no matter what —even if he had to kill to do so! Don't fight him." He put his hands on my shoulders. "You will lose. He wants to kill you, Victor. He is waiting for you. I am all you have now. I am your last and only hope. Trust me…or die like the others."

I dropped to my knees, weeping into my hands. "Oh God," I heard myself whispering. "Oh God, Mother. Oh my God, my family. I am alone forever! Don't let me die. Please, don't let me die."

I couldn't stop weeping. My face was flushed, and I gasped for breath. I found comfort in the arms of this stranger as I cried like a child against his chest, gripping the cloth of his shirt with my fingernails.

My family was dead—my beautiful mother, Charles, and David…my baby brother. My hard-working, wonderful father—all gone—all dead. All I could do was cry and cry and cry!

My sobbing eventually ceased, making me feel very weak and sleepy.

The stranger leaned over me. "I must ask you a question, Victor."

I stared into his eyes, waiting for the beautiful sound of his voice once again.

"Can you endure eternity?"

I narrowed my eyes. "What?"

"Can you endure eternity?" he repeated.

"What are you speaking of?" I whispered it, thinking he must be mad.

"Answer the question, young one."

"I don't understand."

"Eternity. To live as you are now for all time, where sickness, death, and time mean nothing to you. Where the world changes but you do not. When there is nothing left to accomplish and nothing more to see, but you are still here—and always will be."

"You *are* mad."

"No. I am sane. I am just not...not—"

"Not what?"

He grinned, revealing his monstrous teeth. "Human."

I think he noticed the crazed look of confusion in my eyes. He knelt down to meet my gaze.

"As I told you," he began, "I am flesh and blood but not human. I cannot die, cannot fall ill, will never grow old. I can hear your words before you speak them. I can move at a speed no man can master."

"What are you?"

"Don't be frightened. I am a creature of the damned, a creature of the night, but I swear to you now, Victor, I am not evil, and I mean you no harm! I love you, Victor. I want to help you."

"You're a…monster."

"That doesn't matter," he whispered. "Just wait. I will explain to you soon enough, but you must believe me. Did you not notice? Your wound…it is healed."

Chapter Two

VAMPIRE, devil, monster—so many horrible words came to mind. He had a wonderful, terrible power to heal me with his blood! He was cold and hard like stone. He was beautiful and flawless like an angel, but he possessed fangs like a devil. He had saved me, but he had done so with blood. I could not decide whether to trust him or run the other direction as fast as I could.

He stared at me for long moments, just studying me as if I appeared to him just as strange as he appeared to me. How did he pass along every day without drawing attention to himself? How could anybody believe he was human?

He leaned in toward me. "Can you endure eternity?" he whispered in my ear.

Those same words again. I couldn't respond. I still didn't understand what he was asking of me. He leaned in closer until I could feel his breath upon my neck.

"Eternity," he whispered.

The press of his teeth against my skin should have ignited panic, but instead, I felt myself freeze, unable to move. He pushed through, sinking his teeth deep into my neck. I tried to scream, but my body didn't respond.

When he pulled away, I was finally able to move, and the panic slithered into me. I prepared to scream, but he clamped his hand around my throat until I couldn't breathe.

He released me, and I was met with wrenching coughs. Tears stained my cheeks, and the panic was still paralyzing me.

"Are you going to kill me?" I choked out, almost too frightened of the answer.

"I'm going to save you," he whispered.

"Please, tell me the truth. What are you?"

"I told you. It is all true, Victor. I am immortal. I am two hundred and seventeen years old. I know no limitations. The laws of time and mortality do not apply to me. But I am alone, Victor."

I stared at him for a moment, searching for the right words. "You drink blood. You're a—"

"Vampire."

Now the panic I was feeling hit me full force, and I stood from the cot I was lying on, ready to flee. This monster brought me here to feed on me and roam the land, infecting all with his vile disease.

As I began to run, he appeared in front of me, lifting me from the ground and plopping me back on the cot. I scrambled to my feet, but he pushed me down again.

"Relax, child." His voice was calm, which only frightened me more. "I will never force you, Victor. It is your choice, but I cannot let you leave until you understand what I am asking of you."

I tried to speak but had no words.

"I am asking you one simple thing. Can you endure eternity, or can you not?"

"I don't know."

"Think about it, child. Everlasting life. To be free from pain. You will have strength, power, beauty, and riches beyond your wildest dreams."

"No more pain?"

"No more crop work, no more laboring under the hot sun. The night will be your companion and your love. A new world with no misery, no regret…"

"No pain?"

"No pain. You will live your dreams, Victor."

I stared, suddenly transfixed. This was my choice. "To be like you?"

He smiled. "To become like me. To be born of the night. To be an immortal, supernatural wonder!"

"No more pain," I whispered. *No more pain.*

I felt a sense of tiredness come over me and found myself slipping into unconsciousness. The stranger stroked my golden hair and spoke to me words I do not remember. I closed my eyes, humming sweet tunes of my mother's music. I could almost hear her speaking to me. Perhaps I was already asleep.

He tilted his head and brushed my hair from my neck. He poked through the wounds, and the blood drew quickly.

I heard the loud pounding of a bass drum, quick and hard. The sound became faster as he continued to widen the wound with his teeth. I realized this sound was my heartbeat, slowing until I thought for sure I would die.

"Can you endure eternity?"

"Yes," I cried out, or I had tried to.

I watched in fascination as he broke the vein in his wrist and pressed it against my lips.

The drumming sound came again, followed by another, faster than my own. As I drank, my pulse quickened until they were beating in perfect unison.

When he drew away again, I felt that by some alien force, all of my insides were being ripped out of me, felt as if wild beasts were clawing at my body, and I screamed and writhed on the floor.

"Don't be afraid," I heard him say. "Your body is dying. It's only your humanity. Don't fight it."

I tried to do as he said, but I was afraid—very afraid. If I could imagine what dying was like—this would be it. I reminded myself of life everlasting, of a way to escape the grief of losing my family, as a way to avenge them. Yes. This was what I wanted.

I held my breath, not letting myself scream. I could feel my heart pounding in my chest; I could feel the pulse in every limb of my body. I felt as if I were under water but didn't need to hold my breath. Something was breathing for me. It was him! I had everything now, though ghastly—absolutely wonderful.

I knew him now without him speaking a word. I knew this creature. I knew his name was Daniel, and I knew I loved him, though I could not explain why.

As the pain in my body diminished, I felt a tingling numbness in my limbs. It was curious in a way and pleasant.

"Follow me," said Daniel, softly taking my hand. "For the first night, you will be on your own."

"What?" I halted, gripping his hand. "You can't leave me."

"Don't fear. I will return. You will have all you need."

I tried to protest but was too distraught and distracted staring at my hands and arms, marveling at the feel of my canines, now elongated and sharp like his, and gazing in awe at the way he did not look so different to me anymore.

He *was* just a man with black hair and incredibly dark, luminous eyes beneath thick yet perfectly shaped eyebrows. He smiled, and I could see creases in his face and the pores in his skin. I could hear the blood pumping through his body. He was a monster filled with my very own blood, and now he was leading me somewhere through a hallway and up a long, cruel flight of stairs.

Now I saw where I would be—alone through the day.

Chapter Three

I WAS unable to speak at first.

"Here is where you must conceal yourself from the sunlight," he said. "Do you understand, Victor? The sun will destroy you."

I nodded. "I understand."

I wasn't being entirely honest. I didn't quite understand anything. Now I had to hide from the beauty of the sunlight? I had already lost so much, and the pain of it slithered its way into my chest. I gulped, trying not to let it show.

I glanced at Daniel and back at the coffin at his feet. "Where will you go?"

"Don't worry about that. You will be fine. I promise. Just whatever you do, keep away from the sun."

"I will."

"Farewell."

He was gone before I could blink, and I marveled at his skill. I opened the coffin, and a ping of anxiety hit me when I realized it took only a fraction of my strength. I felt not like the Victor Miller I thought I was. I began to weep, burying my face in my hands, allowing myself to feel everything now that I was alone.

I glanced at my hands and cried out in horror and disgust at the sight of blood running through my fingers. I pressed my fingers to my eyelids, fearing my eyes were injured, but there was no pain. I had stopped crying now, and the blood had ceased. I inhaled deeply, checking again that my eyes weren't damaged.

All right. I weep blood now. That's new.

Before the sun had even begun to rise, I decided to hide myself. I didn't want to take any chances. I stepped inside, trembling at the thought. A cracking sound echoed through the chamber, and I gasped, peering down at what I had stepped on.

I thought for a moment I had broken a mirror, but it couldn't have been a mirror, for it is said creatures of the damned do not have reflections. Even through the cracks in the glass, I could clearly see that the image was not me.

It was a young man with almost glowing, sunlit hair and eyes of deep amber. I smiled. The image did too. I moved my hair behind my ear. The image did too. I gasped, dropping the mirror to the floor. The face that stared back was my own—all white, bloodless, and frightened. A sense of anger bubbled up from inside me, and I pounded the mirror with my fists. There was no pain and no blood, just a lot of broken glass.

I could already feel thirst coming over me, but the sun was rising, and I was more than exhausted.

When I awoke, I was very thirsty and at first unaware of where I was, but as soon as I gained full consciousness, it all flooded back to me, and I wept again. So many times had I cried since I had been in the arms of that monster. I still didn't understand what this little room was or why the room below it was just as empty.

Daniel hadn't come. I was still alone and quite helpless. Each moment was as if I were reborn. I wasn't Victor Miller anymore. No—I had been recreated into a creature of the greatest fascination. I had a terrible thirst in my body I had never felt before; it wasn't like mortal pain or mortal hunger at all. It was something more. It was intense almost, but I enjoyed the pain in a way. I savored it, loving the thought of how amazing and suddenly magical life seemed. Though this was ghastly, there was also so much beauty and power.

I walked down the steps, very frightened of being alone. I heard voices, and I called out to Daniel. The voices were strange. They were human voices, of course, and it was a mumble of words and sounds that had no meaning to me; it was as if hundreds of people were all trying to speak to me at once.

I cried out, but it didn't stop. I sank to my knees, covering my ears with my hands. Calmness came over me as the voices faded. I realized I was on the floor, where I had been the last minutes I had been alive. I lay there and wept. I had so many questions. Why could I hear these voices in my head? Why was it so hard not to listen? Why did I have a reflection?

My body ached from hunger, and blood dripped from my mouth. I realized I had been biting into my lip. I ran my tongue along a fang. Yes, perfectly sharp.

I forced myself to my feet, groaning. I found the door leading out of the room where the scent of mortals flooded my nostrils. The voices were gone, but they kept coming back. I pushed them from my mind until they were no more than a soft hum. I could smell human blood. I could smell their life, and I craved it. I had to feed. There was no more to it. I could think of nothing else.

I had to feed. I *had* to. There was nothing more to it! I looked at the door, guessing Daniel had built this tiny house himself. Where was my master now? I opened the door, not liking the creaking sound that echoed through the room. I stepped into the night, realizing the house stood in the middle of a forest. I walked until I came to the darkened streets where people wandered about, having a late meal or an evening outing. I guess I was a bit of an early riser—the sky was still blue.

My mouth tinged with the need for them—all the beautiful humans. I walked the streets, in search of blood but keeping my senses alert for Daniel as well. I found my victim for the night, chosen at random I must admit—a boy with tight blond curls and blue eyes. He almost approached me, perhaps held in curiosity by the monstrous way I looked, so cold and hungry, so horribly hideous.

I stepped closer to him, and I sensed his fear. It was thrilling. Yes, he was terrified, but before he could run, I had him pulled into an alley, in my arms, drained of his sweet blood—so soft and hot through my body, not like the blood of my master but more innocent and pure. I closed my eyes, savoring each moment of pleasure and delight the liquid sent through me.

Guilt overflowed inside me, but I pushed it away. I must be strong. I must accept what I am. It was the only way to avenge my family. I was afraid Daniel may never return, and I would be forced to discover these things on my own. Everything looked different now. The long dark streets weren't so dark. The people seemed to move even when they didn't; I could see the life in them even as they were still. I could hear their thoughts and words from the other side of the world if I wished. I felt the strength Daniel had released into me. I reveled in it. For now, I was happy but still without a master.

Chapter Four

HE DID RETURN TO ME, surprised to see me so strong and unafraid. I had risen with him by my side, and as soon as my eyes met his, I fell into his arms.

He laughed softly. "I told you to be patient, and you were."

"But I was frightened, Master," I whispered. "So very, very frightened!" I buried my head in his chest. He softly pushed me forward, still smiling. His eyes were so dark, so deep, layered with knowledge and secrets.

"I saw you," he started quietly. "I watched you take down that boy last night. You were amazing, Victor."

I smiled. "His blood was like a mystery made liquid. Something intangible, like…time…or…space."

He laughed under his breath. "Yes. It is remarkable, isn't it? I made a good choice."

He stroked my hair, moving it behind my ears and smoothing it upon my head. He brushed every strand away from my face so he could stare at me. He looked deep into my eyes, smiling as if he were looking at an angel or a ghost

—something he had never seen before. In those moments, I had forgotten I was just a boy, just Victor Miller. When I realized this, it alarmed me. I *was* just Victor Miller, wasn't I?

"You are so much more than that now."

I gasped, backing away. A smile crept onto my face as the initial shock subsided. "Don't do that."

Daniel smiled. "Apologies. You are more, Victor—more than you have ever been before. You are strong. You are without torment, without regret."

"I don't understand. Torment? Regret? Why should I feel such feelings?"

"Many creatures do. Many have pain in their hearts… guilt…regret."

I remember the pang of guilt that struck me after my first kill. I remembered how I had pushed it away, accepting the unalterable ways of my new life. "Animals kill. God kills for heaven's sake. Why should *I* feel guilt?"

"Wise beyond your age, Victor."

"I do want to know, Master. Are we…?"

"Evil?"

"Yes."

"Evil is what you make it. Evil is a point of view. You are a predator, Victor. There is no evil in that. You said as much yourself."

I nodded. "Why do I have a reflection?"

He chuckled. "Oh—you found the hand mirror."

"Broke it, actually."

"Most of the stories you have heard are no more than superstitions. Forget them. I will teach you all you need to know. I must ask you. Does your thirst for revenge still compel you?"

"Every moment of my existence." I turned away with a sigh. "The Cornallys will die. They will, and the land will be burned."

He placed a hand on my shoulder. "Not just yet. Your time will come, but let me first show you all our world has to offer."

The time passed quickly while I was learning with my master by my side. He watched in fascination at each new discovery as though he had never before seen what our kind could do. I adored Daniel's child-like innocence that shone through him; even when he spoke like an elder and taught like an elder, he loved me in the pure way of a child.

Over the time while I waited to take my revenge, Daniel taught me the arts of literature so I could write my poetry in a journal rather than just reciting it.

There was nothing in the world now that didn't hold some kind of magic, some mystery, nothing that couldn't arouse my curiosity, my fascination. The nights were long and filled with the greatest of sport. My first meal, as I had said, was chosen at random, which I soon learned was the mistake I made. Not only did we choose our victims carefully, we dressed and spoke for the occasion as well.

My master had found a grave where we rested. I—like most children—didn't understand why we couldn't conceal ourselves from the sun inside a house, beneath the warm blankets of a bed, but I didn't ask him about it. The poetry in my mind ran deeper and darker than it ever had before, and when the beautiful words fell from my lips—for the first time, I was not scolded. Daniel loved the way I spoke when I told him about the music of the stars and the silvery, milky voice of the moon.

"The night summons," I said, "begging for another night when our beauty shines beneath her."

He smiled. "You truly *are* a poet."

"No. No, I only wish I were."

"Oh, but you are, Victor. Truly."

That night passed quickly, and before I had even realized I had risen, I was back in the grave beside Daniel, filled with hot, mortal blood.

It would not be honest of me to say I loved killing. I enjoyed the sport and the power, yes, but I was also afflicted with a sense of empathy when my victims begged for the mercy I could not show them. I tried to hunt for only the evil, and John Cornally and his bastard family would be next.

"Come now," Daniel whispered. "I will show you how to be the child I have made you into. Don't be afraid." He placed his arm around my waist. "I won't let you go."

I felt myself rise up from the ground, and I shrieked, gripping him tightly. I heard him laugh.

"It's all right," he said, almost playfully. "You're not going to fall."

He released me on the roof of a house, much like my own used to be.

"Can you sense them, Victor? The humans?"

"I can."

"Do you wish to take these mortals?"

"May I?"

"They deserve to die in your arms."

I crawled through the window and found a sleeping girl, not much older than myself. Good God, what would this human blood be like? Not monster blood but this sweet, innocent blood? I approached her, and without waking her, I lifted her head from the pillow, feeling her dark curly locks of hair wrap and fall around my fingers. I tilted her head and sank my cruel teeth into her neck. I could taste the salt of her flesh and the metal in her blood. I pulled away, savoring the pleasure of the feed. I leaned back against the wall and closed my eyes. I felt weightless, soft, dizzy. I growled quietly from the ecstasy and the strength. I couldn't get enough; I wanted more, *needed* more!

And I got more—more and more until I was past satisfied, and when the light came creeping over the mountainside, Daniel took me home.

"Sleep now," he said, "and when you awake, you will almost be ready to take your revenge."

I smiled and fell asleep, warm from the night's feed.

"The time will come," he told me. "Save them for a night when you can truly enjoy them."

"The Cornallys will die if it's the last thing I ever do," I whispered as if speaking to myself.

"It won't be the last thing, Victor. When you are strong enough, you will take your revenge. I promise you this is the best way to do things."

I nodded, slowly bringing my gaze back into his dark eyes. I would await the Cornallys' murder with as much patience as I could manage. The days were sleepless, and the nights were long. Every moment I grew stronger, but it wasn't until the night came that I realized it. Daniel told me not to be a coward. He said those who weep are cowards. He made me strong—he made me cold. I felt compassionless to anything and everything besides my dead family. The

Cornallys were next, no more waiting, no more patience. The time…was now!

I walked beside Daniel to the Cornallys' little house. It was a lot like mine was, so it was quite easy to find the rooms. I knew I had to take Mrs. Cornally; although I knew she was innocent, it was for that very reason she must die painlessly, lest the pain in her heart from the loss of her beloved son and husband would be unbearable. I took her silently. Then I moved to Mr. Cornally. I woke him up slowly.

"Hello, Mr. Cornally," I said devilishly, smiling at him, revealing my fangs. He sprang up and leaned back against the headboard. Sweat formed in beads upon his forehead, his body trembling. I could smell his sweat, his skin, and it was making me sick.

"V-Victor?"

"You recognize me," I whispered. "Even in the dark. I'm not surprised. After you tried so hard to kill me, you should recognize me."

"P-Please," he started, shaking so fiercely I could hear his teeth chattering. "I…don't understand."

"I guess you got the Miller family land you wanted so badly."

"What are you talking about?"

"I'm talking about you murdering my family."

Silence.

"No more pain," I whispered.

I tore into his neck without mercy. I could hear the strained screams he was unable to force from his throat.

Now for John Jr. Now this would be sweet! I found his room and woke him.

"Father?" he questioned, rubbing his eyes.

"Not exactly."

"The voice," he whispered as though I couldn't hear him.

"Yes, you know the voice," I said, stepping closer. I leaned in toward him. "And you know the face."

He gasped, backing up, holding the blanket to his chin, his eyes widened until they looked far too large for his face.

"Victor?" he choked. "It can't be."

"And why is that? Because I'm supposed to be dead? Because you must have hit me with the knife you threw? Tell me, John, who'd you kill first, my mother or David? Tell me, John. Are you frightened?"

"I am frightened, Victor."

"Because you're guilty."

"Because you're frightening me."

I stepped closer, and he seemed to notice the change in my skin, in my eyes, noticed I did not look alive.

"You…you're"—he swallowed, choking on the last word —"dead."

"Oh, is that so?" I laughed. "And I've risen from my grave to take my revenge?"

"I believe that is exactly what you've done."

"Perhaps, but that does not change your fate."

He was scrambling now, pushing himself against the headboard and searching for something, anything to hit me with.

"Don't be afraid, John. Say a prayer."

"If you take one step closer, I swear I will call my father."

"Call your father," I said, stepping closer, "but I wouldn't count on him hearing you."

"My God," he answered almost in disgust. "You didn't."

"Find out. Call your father. Scream, weep, beg for mercy —just like my brother did."

He was silent.

"Go ahead," I whispered. "Scream—I want you to."

"No," he growled. "I will not scream for you. Your father was a fool. He was warned and warned."

"Perhaps he was a fool, but your father is a murderer, as are you, and Heaven does not hold a place for murderers. You die now."

And he screamed.

As soon as the blood started flowing, I learned something I did not expect. John's very last thoughts were not, *Lord, forgive me* or *Lord, I beg your mercy* or even confessions of love for the Lord. His very last thoughts were, *Victor, I deserve to die, but before I do, I want you to know that I am sorry for bringing this pain upon you—forgive me.* And with those last thoughts, he was gone, and I…was happy.

The land was burned along with the essence of my family. I wept openly, and Daniel did not scold me. He handed me a blackened piano key he had found in the ruins of the house. I tearfully took it and embraced him.

I departed back home, knowing I would sleep well, having my revenge satiated. When I slept, I dreamed of my family. They thanked me for bringing them justice. And my beloved mother, she smiled at me, and through her eyes, I could almost feel that music emanating from her, that soft, beautiful piano music that always made me recite pretty words to go with it. My dreams were comforting, and when I awoke to see Daniel, he saw my happiness.

"You received what you wanted. Are you happier now?"

"I am."

He embraced me, and I could feel his soft, dark hair upon my cheek. As the nights passed, each new evening was filled with new discoveries. My powers were incredible, and they did not frighten me. But as I was happy, I was growing very *un*happy. I killed the Cornallys, and for what? To bring comfort to myself? My family was still dead, the only difference was that now the Cornallys…were dead too.

Chapter Five

"MOTHER, I WANT TO ACT."

"And wouldn't you make a lovely Romeo—or Puck, maybe."

I choked back my tears when I thought of my mother and the fact that even now that I was given a new life, I could never be that beautiful boy on stage, dressed in a velvet costume, reciting Shakespearian lines. All I wanted was to act and to write poetry. I knew I shouldn't tell Daniel how I felt, but I cried to him as a child would to a father. He didn't berate me, but he called me a coward.

"Too many tears, my love."

"I want to act, Daniel. It's my deepest desire, implanted since the day I was born—I want to act! It would ease my pain to know I can still be that boy I always dreamed of being."

"I know," Daniel whispered. "It's all right. Do you not see?"

I only stared.

"Do you not see?"

"Do I not see what, Master?"

He sighed.

"I don't understand."

"The murder of the Cornallys was the greatest act of the century, Adorato. Don't you see? The world is a theater, and you…are the star!"

I mirrored his smile. "Yes. It was an amazing act, wasn't it? I *am* an actor."

"You always have been, my love."

"Have I?"

"You never saw it, Adorato, but I did. I see the way your dreams seep through you like your poetry."

I smiled. "I *can* act…?"

"No," he answered, grinning. "You *do* act."

"So perhaps every hunt, Master, I am a different person."

"Of course. Take the role, Victor. Who will you be tonight?"

"Perhaps it depends on the victim."

"As it should."

"Thank you, Master."

Knowing my one true passion could be mine took away some of the sadness I was drowning in. Not only could I act, I could do it in a way no one else could.

Each night, I would be a different man in a different costume. A different character would commit every evil deed and every delicious kill. Daniel was right; the world was a theater, a stage, and the crowd was cheering for me.

Each and every evening was a different act for me. It was so magical! I could be a regretful predator, a heartless killer, a madman, a mistaken man. And all of those beautiful mortals—Lord, how I loved watching them die in my arms. I killed only those who were unwanted; although occasionally, I couldn't resist the taste of innocence, such as the boy I had taken down the first night or the pretty girl asleep in her bed. The way they were so loved added an even better thrill and taste as well.

I loved Daniel as much as I loved my family. He was all I had now. Though I loved him, I worried at times about the things he did. It started the day he murdered the Fosters—mother, father, and two children, Michael and Anna. The family was young and wealthy.

I knew he had done it for me, as he had forged the father's will stating that everything was to be left to his "dear friend, Victor Miller." Of course, this home was quite far from my own, so nobody knew who I was.

I didn't care who was actually supposed to have the money and estate of Mr. Foster. I only cared that it was mine now.

Some people had asked me why no one in the Foster family had ever mentioned my name. I said that Mr. Foster and I had a business relationship, turned personal.

Mr. Foster wasn't rich by his own work but by the work of his dead uncle as far as I heard, but I have little knowledge of the situation, and I really didn't care.

The house was beautiful. It was a real castle made of brick and stone, with tall towers and peaks that pierced the gray clouds. I smiled and fell into Daniel's arms.

"It's ours now, Victor. *Yours* now."

I had a house, a real house, and no field to labor in under the hot, burning sun. The rooms were big and well lit, full of beautiful furnishings and a bed for me and one for my master as well.

Daniel closed the curtains of the front room and signaled

me to the chair opposite of him. "There are so many things I have to share with you."

"Where did you come from?"

He laughed. "Hmmm, Russia," he answered, closing his eyes. "I came from Russia. I was born in Italy but taken by my captors to Russia."

I smiled and whispered, "Russia."

"The men who made me—I didn't know them very well. They left me when I was only very young."

"Left you? But—"

"I don't know why," he answered. "I truly don't. Let me explain to you, Victor, please."

"I would never tell you no, Daniel."

I kept my eyes on Daniel as he spoke.

"As I had said," he started precisely, "my captors left me when I was very young, but there was one man who took care of me. His name was Ashman. He was an Egyptian and a vampire of many centuries, reaching all the way back before the birth of Moses. He would come to me and take me hunting.

"His face was expressionless, like a statue of white stone. He almost seemed to float more than actually step, and I marveled at his skill from humanlike to ghostlike. He confused me, I must admit. His life was like a secret he would never tell. He wasn't supposed to become a vampire. He never intended on it, but Ashman had been created in secret. His creation was a mystery as well. I didn't know his maker.

"My creation is vague, for my captors never cared much

for me. I always thought they had made me simply because of the love they had for their power. What I do remember is lying in that warm bed, dying, drained almost completely of blood. I was beyond all suffering by then—I couldn't feel much. Then suddenly, I was filled with blood once more, not by the man who took it away but by Thaddeus, the man who stood beside him—Thaddeus and his companion Eric. I cannot recall exactly what it felt like—only that I didn't understand what was happening, and it hurt, and the more I fought, the more it hurt. When at last I gave up, I found there was less pain, and when it was over, I suddenly felt love for my captors. They had snatched me from my home and my family—which I sadly do not remember—and took me deep into the heart of Russia in the year 1522 and created me as Daniel Sarcova—vampire child. Eric took my life, and Thaddeus gave it back. Centuries passed before I had the strength to create, for my own blood was not given back to me, so when the time was right, I chose you, Victor Miller."

"Wait…so I am your first child?"

He nodded. "I lacked the strength until now."

"And your life?" I asked curiously.

He shook his head. "You may learn of it later, but not now, Victor. I'm not ready yet."

My home was beautiful, and I couldn't have asked for more, but all the same—there was something missing. It wasn't until Daniel found it that I realized it. I came home one evening from a night's feed to see my master standing at the doorway.

"Victor!" he cried. "You'll never believe what I have found!"

There wasn't much of a response from me; I didn't know what he was saying.

"Come and see."

He led me into Anna Foster's old bedroom, but it wasn't empty.

"What have you done?" I asked, but I was smiling because he was smiling, and that always meant something good.

"You can see her," he said. "Go ahead."

In Anna's bed was a tiny child, asleep, with a doll nestled tightly in her arms. My smile was stripped away, and I slowed my movement and my breathing. Suddenly, I was aware of everything. All the things I was looking at appeared as though I was looking at them for the first time. I knelt down beside the bed and stroked the child's hair, her deep auburn hair. Her rounded eyes were closed, and a breath escaped her pink lips—a gentle mortal breath.

"Daniel," I whispered, "she's…human."

"Yes," he answered, smiling. "Yes, she is."

"Are you going to let her stay that way?"

"The only reason I hadn't made her was for your sake. It all depends on what you want, Adorato."

"I…I want"—I sighed—"I want her to stay. I mean…I want her to stay here as mortal or immortal."

He smiled. "We can make her for us, Victor. Only…I don't think I want to."

"Why?"

"She was not chosen by me. I am just afraid that it may be a mistake. Children are…complicated. When turned, they have a tendency for violence and recklessness. We have no conception of what she may be capable of. I did not choose her to be one of us. I took her to save her."

"To save her? Where did you find her, Master?"

"Alone. Alone in the streets."

"And her family?"

"Dead, I imagine. I know from her thoughts that her mother is dead. I don't know about her father."

"I share her pain." I continued to stroke her hair, realizing I shared the same loss this child had faced, the loss of a beloved mother. I stayed there beside her, studying her locks of reddened hair. "What's her name, Daniel?"

No answer.

I turned to see my master was no longer standing at the doorway.

"Anna," I whispered, smiling. "Your name will be Anna."

She waked under my touch, and her pretty blue eyes locked onto mine. She gasped, springing up in the bed.

"Shh," I whispered. "I am here to take care of you."

"Who are you? Where is my mother?" Her voice was so tiny and frail. I sensed her terror.

"Shh. Mother has left you with me. You're with me now."

"But I—where…?"

"What's your name? Where did you live?"

Still no response.

"Please don't be frightened," I coaxed. "Please…what's your name?"

"She doesn't know," I heard Daniel say. "She doesn't remember anything but her mother. I found her unconscious on the ground. Amnesia, I'm guessing. Victor, take care of her."

"I need to turn her!" I cried. "She needs me."

"It wouldn't be right. She's far too young."

"Please, Daniel, you have to help me. I haven't the courage to do it."

"And I haven't the foolishness."

"Daniel, what will happen to her if we leave her mortal to stay with us?" I left her side and approached Daniel and whispered quietly so as to not frighten her with our conversation. "What will happen when we let her watch us prey off her kind? Fear and confusion will be all she possesses. Then when she runs away, you'll have to pray she finds somebody to care for her before she dies."

"Victor..." He sighed and bowed his head. "You certainly have a love like no other."

"And you?"

"We must remain in the shadows, Victor. She shouldn't be made one of us. I'm warning you now, my child."

"You said it was my choice."

"I never thought you would make this one."

"It's the only way."

"Is this truly what you want?"

"It's not only about me."

He sighed. "All right. Under one condition."

I waited.

"Give yourself some time. Get to know her true mortal soul before you decide to destroy it."

"What we are—she cannot understand as a human."

He nodded. "I understand your concern, but it is still best to wait. She will understand everything when the time comes, and all that fear and confusion will dissipate."

I nodded. "All right. I'll wait."

Chapter Six

DANIEL HAD A WRITER FRIEND, probably somebody he had met at a café or on the streets between kills. His name was Charles. I hated that name. Whenever Daniel spoke of him, I saw my brother's face and blinked away my tears.

Daniel had started hunting alone. The only time he took me with him was when I begged him to. I hated being alone.

Charles never liked me for some reason, but whenever he stopped by for evening visits, he never gave Anna a moment's peace.

Eventually, we saw less and less of Charles until he ceased to stop by altogether.

"You killed him, didn't you?" I said to Daniel one evening after a hunt.

He smiled, almost as if he didn't hear me. "It was for the best," he answered with a sigh.

The hatred in his heart confused me. He never even showed an ounce of love or affection to Anna. She never spoke of it. She never asked what we were, but I knew we frightened her. The expressions of fear on her face sickened me, tortured me, and Daniel knew it. He saw it every night.

"I love her with all the humanity I possess," I told him.

"And that is your first mistake. You should possess no humanity at all. That is not the case, for I see it—the love. You lavish affection on her. You kill shop keepers to bring things home for Anna. Why do you do that?"

"Is it so strange for me to bring gifts home for my child?"

"Your child?"

"What else is she, Daniel? She's here. We care for her."

He didn't respond. It didn't matter. Anna was my daughter. We shared a companionship and a love that Daniel was not included in.

Anna was a quiet, intelligent child with enormous, beaming eyes that burned into my flesh, and at times, I wanted her, wanted to take her blood into mine and let her die in my arms with love as her last thoughts. But I didn't. Instead, I painted flowers on the walls of her bedroom, taught her how to play the piano so I could listen to my mother's old music. I taught her how to set a table and told her that someday she would go to school. Her eyes were filled with secrets—secrets of questions she would never ask.

Daniel had kept his promise to me. He let me know her mortal soul and then set out to destroy it. I didn't want him to make her one of us anymore, but I knew it had to be that way. I truly wanted him to let her grow up even if that meant that someday I would lose her. I wanted her to be mortal. I loved seeing the life in her flesh. I loved hearing her mortal blood rushing through her veins. I loved listening to her heartbeat against me as she embraced me and slept near me. Most of all, I loved cooking for her, making sweet mortal meals for her. It was over now. She would soon forget the six years of her mortal life and remember every thought and feeling ever created in her mind as a vampire. Daniel would make her, and I couldn't stop him. I didn't want to. I knew what had to be done. It's what I had wanted in the first place anyway.

I watched intensely as he knelt beside her and told her that he was going to give her a gift. He told her someday she would better understand his gift. I watched in horror as his two sharpened fangs pricked her neck. A moan escaped her lips as if she was trying to weep but couldn't. Her hand was outstretched as if gripping something that wasn't there. I extended my arm and let her take my hand. Her tiny fingers strengthened an unnatural grasp against my knuckles. She squeezed my fingers, letting Daniel take her, and at last her hand fell limp, but I didn't let it go. It was as if time wasn't there, as if it didn't exist and never did exist, and I stared at her for what seemed like hours, unconscious of everything but the tiny mortal hand almost hidden within my own. And abruptly, from a force I had forgotten about, the cold white hand had life in it once more and moved across my fingers, and tiny little arms wrapped around my neck as a silver voice whispered, "I love you."

It was at this moment I noticed a ghastly yet beautiful transformation in Anna. Her large blue eyes had age in them now—knowledge and secrets. She smiled at me almost as if the six years of her mortal life were gone.

Anna grew with us as part of us and grew into an incredible killer. She found death quickly and no longer depended on me to bring her home pretty dresses or games. It saddened me that Anna didn't need me the way she used to; she took what she wanted—always.

I felt I had lost Anna in a part of me that always held her. She didn't feed alone very often; she was always with Daniel and me. But I hated the way she looked at me, the way she loathed my mortal expressions of pain when I thought of the murder I had committed and the family I had lost.

During the good times with Anna, she remained the child to me that she had always been, but it was different for Daniel. To Daniel, she was more a partner in crime; to me, she was a costar, a beautiful child who acted alongside me while we hunted. She had a strong love for Daniel that she never had before, and both of us were "Father" now.

"She knows," Daniel had said to me.

"And when she asks, who will tell her?"

No response.

I sighed. Someday, Anna would ask us the same questions we all do. *What have you done to me? What are you? What are we?* But the years passed, and not a word slipped from her lips about her creation. Perhaps the knowledge and wisdom Daniel possessed had answered her questions during her transition. It was as if she did not know life could be any different. Her humanity was fading, and she never knew a time when she was not the ageless vampire child.

"A legend!" Will said with a smile.

Victor looked at him passively—questioningly. He laughed under his breath. "Perhaps...but this is more than a legend. It is a true tale."

"And it is enchanting," William answered, his smile squinting his green eyes.

Victor stared at the face of young William for a moment, studying his features—the masculine build of his jaw, his large green eyes tinted with blue.

He broke his gaze and sighed, slouching back in his chair.

"I'm not sure I understand," William said, staring at Victor as though he were wounded in some way. "You speak of things I could only ever hope to comprehend, and yet you are miserable. You are consumed by your grief. Why is that?"

"I'll get to that. You'll understand."

As time passed, Daniel's attention seemed to be waning, and he was very cold toward me. Anna loved me as she always had, but Daniel had told me he hated her, reminding me he warned me her creation would have been a ghastly mistake. Perhaps he was right, but at the time, I felt an obligation to protect Anna and to care for her, making sure that no harm would ever come to her. But Daniel didn't want anything to do with the child, anything at all.

I clearly remember the night when she finally spoke the words I had been waiting so long to hear.

"Tell me, Father," she started. "Tell me why it is that you refer to the outsiders as mortals and us as vampires. What are we?"

I wasn't sure how to answer as I was still unsure whether or not I understood it myself. "We are immortal. Nightly predators that feed on mortals for our benefit. Not that it matters, Anna."

She nodded. "I've understood that for a long time."

"What do you mean?"

"I know what we are. I wanted to know if you would tell me."

"I will tell you anything you want to know. I love you more than all the world. You know that."

I felt a shudder emanating from her. I could feel her grief, her confusion. I stared into her eyes, watching them gather the light.

She slouched onto the floor, resting her chin in her drawn-up knees. "Tell me again."

"Tell you what?"

"Tell me you love me."

"Oh, Anna. Of course I love you. How could you ever think differently?"

"Because of the pain you always hide from me. Because of all the secrets. Because you never speak of what it was like."

"About what was like?"

"Being human," she whispered. "Being loved."

"I'm sorry, Anna." I kneeled beside her on the floor. "Truly I am. I was waiting for you to ask. I did not realize it was your right to know all along."

"I love you too, Father. But Daniel wants me gone."

"Why do you say that?"

"Because I look into his mind when he sleeps."

I was stunned for a moment, not realizing she knew how to do something like that. "He doesn't understand, but I believe he loves you."

She shook her head. "I know he wants me gone."

"Everything will be fine, Anna. I promise."

"I admire your faith."

I looked away as she left the room, still feeling her emotions coursing through me.

"I take care of her because she cannot take care of herself," Daniel said, stepping into the room. "You know this. But I do not want her here anymore. Do something with her, will you?"

"And what do you suggest I do? You're the one who did this to her. This is your fault."

He ignored my accusation. "Just occupy her. She is nothing but a burden."

I scowled at him. "You're so cold."

Anna had always been a lovely child, but there was something about her that tortured Daniel—the way she looked at him, the way she mocked his mistakes. It was more than I myself could bear. I think he believed if he convinced himself he hated her, her hatred for him wouldn't pain him.

Daniel had a way of showing his strength through cruelty. Anna and I were cowards—weak creatures with no right to have him love us; that's what he told us…every night.

Thirty years had passed, and nothing yet had changed. Anna's eyes grew tenser and tenser with her age, and something let me know she was no longer a child.

We were in love as it were, and Daniel seemed sickened by our dancing and singing together in ways we never before had. I remember once walking in on a conversation.

"Do you, Father?" she asked, her face passive and pale.

"There is no reason for me to stay here any longer. I took care of you because you could not take care of yourself, but you have Victor now, so both of you can leave me in peace."

I told Daniel he truly didn't understand—that Anna and I loved him, that we still needed him. He was older and stronger than me, but at times, he seemed so weak. He fell weak whenever Anna stared at him with those big saddened eyes.

"I hate the way you look at me," Anna told me. "The way you have such mortal pain in your eyes."

"I am not mortal," I whispered.

"But I see mortal pain deep within your eyes, Father."

I thought of all the things I had done, the things I had said. My soul ached, and all I longed for was one second where everything was right again, where everything was how it used to be—the three of us as a happy family. Daniel hated me—my love, my master. My family was still dead, and Anna's eyes were still filled with fear of something she would not speak of.

"It isn't mortal pain," I said, "for it cannot be. I am immortal, and so are you."

"I understand that," she answered, wrapping her arms around my neck. I found her on my lap as she had been as a mortal child. "I've understood it for a long time. I have no questions."

"Don't you want to know anything?"

"Just one thing." She dropped her gaze to the floor. "What is that trinket you are always fidgeting with?"

I slipped the piano key into my pocket. "It's nothing. Just something of mortal memory."

"And mortal pain."

I sighed. "So perhaps you're right."

"Daniel will be gone before dusk tomorrow."

"You know this?"

"And so do you."

She was right, of course. I did know, for Daniel was already gone, but we slept as if nothing had changed. When we awoke, we were prepared to leave the place we had spent the last thirty-three years of our lives. We were on our way to a new age, and the land I had always dreamed of was exactly where we planned on going—France. And we did go to France, and there I had found someone who had brought the greatest change to my life as it had been before.

My mind was at peace in that beautiful place and for one reason—Anna. We were the father and daughter of the century, affectionate and tender toward one another, and whatever Anna wanted, Anna got.

Even with the newfound happiness and peace, I longed for someone to guide us as Daniel had. I searched for years, but it seemed hopeless. Perhaps there were no others. Perhaps we were the only ones of our kind.

It was just as I had given up hope that an immortal found *me*.

Chapter Seven

IT WAS at that moment when Will had interrupted Victor's story.

"Could this be a legendary vampire?" he asked, his eyes wide with curiosity and wonder.

"Hold on." Victor laughed, putting up his hand to calm the boy. "First, allow me to back up. I had skipped too far ahead. Allow me to return to the night before Daniel left us."

William nodded.

It was a night that I remember more clearly than most of the nights in my life. He seemed almost sad as he spoke.

"If you go with her," he started, "then you surrender to her charm, her enchantment. She will take you from all paths of reasons and along the path of wild dreams."

"Go with her where?" I yelled.

"Certainly you don't intend on staying here, do you?"

"If you leave, Daniel, then I don't believe I would stay

here. No. But what are you talking about? Surrendering to the path of wild dreams?"

He sighed. "It was nothing. It was a moment of agitation, nothing more. I don't know what I was saying."

"It meant something, Daniel. What?"

"If I wish not to tell you, then why must I?"

"I meant no offense."

"You sicken me! You and your constant dancing with the demon child like it's some sort of mad waltz."

"Why are you saying this?"

"All you do is dance with her as if you were two mortal lovers, but you are not," he spat. "You are not mortal, and you are not normal."

"What are you saying?"

"I'm saying that you and the demon child are a world of trouble entirely by yourselves, and if you do not realize the way you must live, if you do not remember the first lesson, then you are doomed."

"First lesson?"

"That we must be powerful and superior to mortals. Acting as mortals is not acting superior to them. Don't you understand, Victor?"

"But it's all only acting. The world is a theatre, and I am the star."

"Good Lord, Victor! Wake up! Stop with your fantasies and foolish childhood dreams that will never come true. Open your eyes, child. Look in the mirror—something. Do you have any idea what you are? What Anna is?"

"Why are you saying such things? Why are you saying this, Daniel?"

"Answer me!"

"Of course I know what I am! I know what Anna is. You made us this way. But do you know what *you* are?"

He didn't respond, just stared at me almost as if he regretted what he had just said to me.

"Do you? You are my master!" I yelled. "I can't make it without you."

"You can make it without anybody!" he snapped. "I've taught you and Anna all you need to know, and now—you only sicken me."

"How could you do this?" I screamed, suddenly stricken with rage. "How could you make me this way…then abandon me?"

He sighed loudly and stepped into Anna's room. "This room will forever emanate evil. It will forever be filled with anger and hatred toward me, won't it!" he yelled, pointing his finger toward the room and leaning in toward me so I could clearly see the anger in his beautiful eyes.

Was he crying?

"Daniel…"

"It will be filled with the stench of hatred, and all because I cannot stay here any longer!"

"Daniel, please…"

He picked up his bag and slung it onto his back. He put his hand on my shoulder, and as he looked at me, his eyes appeared to sink in sadness.

"Remember, Victor," he started softly, "if ever life becomes unbearable, there is always the rising sun."

I tried to speak, tried to search my mind for something, anything that would make him change his mind.

"Even as you watch me leave you," he started almost sadly, "remember that I will always love you, and someday, I will bring you back to me. Farewell, Victor Miller."

"Daniel! Daniel, wait…" But he was gone before he heard me.

Anna and I slept a few hours later, and when we awoke, we were prepared to leave.

I went to my room and hid my diary along with Anna's in a crevice in the wall and nailed up another board to hide the opening. There was no need to write in little notebooks. I didn't see a reason why anybody would ever want to know the pain that our kind bear. I said a prayer to bless the room and fetched Anna's doll.

"Leave it," she said.

"What?"

"I don't want it." She turned away from it as if the very sight of it pained her. She walked into her room and ran her fingers across the hand-painted flowers. "From my father's beautiful hand," she whispered and sighed. "May this room be forever cursed with my hatred."

"Hatred for what, my love?" I asked in a flat, saddened voice.

"Hatred for the world and for the unfairness of it all, for the death of my mother and yours as well."

"You know…?"

"I knew she was dead," she answered. "Only I do not remember how. I think Daniel may know. I think he feels guilt for something."

"For knowing and not telling."

"Perhaps." She sighed and snatched the doll from my hands. "I want to leave it here." She dropped it upon the bed.

We left the house and stayed in a hotel before booking passage to France. I waited impatiently for the boat to arrive; I wanted to travel the human way with my beautiful, auburn-haired child. I was fearful that if we didn't leave soon, I would never be free of Daniel. I wanted to see him, to touch him, to speak to him. I wanted to so badly. He was my maker and my father. I knew if I didn't get out of there, I would spend the rest of forever—if there is such a thing—searching for him and trying to bring him back to me. But I couldn't do that. I had no choice but to accept the fact that Daniel was gone, and for reasons I couldn't yet understand, he could not return—ever!

It wasn't until at least a day after the land before us had disappeared did I stop weeping. Anna wept too. I held tightly to my piano key and stared into Anna's pretty eyes. I had never seen her cry before, not since she was taken to my home by Daniel, and I was glad as she wept she was silent.

Her tiny white hand was reddened by her tears, which she thankfully did not seem to notice. I held her in my arms and promised her that as soon as we got to France, everything would be better—everything would be all right.

Chapter Eight

THE TIMES WERE INTERESTING. I would like to not delve into the history of those times if you don't mind. I regret thinking of the Napoleonic affairs and the political issues. It pains me.

As I was saying, the times with Anna were great until she seemed to become distant and didn't speak to me as much. I didn't want to talk to her about it for fear I would upset her in some way, but as she continued to become worse about it, I had to ask her.

"Anna," I started softly as if she were still a child, "what's wrong, my love?"

"What do you mean?"

"Why do you seem so full of lament? What is it that's hurting you?"

She sighed. "I just want to know why you didn't tell me, Father."

"Didn't tell you what?"

"Oh God, Victor, please don't do this to me! You knew

what Daniel had done. You knew the very day he did it. You knew!"

I felt my limbs begin to tremble. A nervous sickness grew in the pit of my stomach. I knew it was the hateful murder of the Foster family Daniel had committed. But she took another path.

"How could he have done this to me?" she asked, sinking her voice to a whisper and bowing her head. The hotel room was cold that night, and I embraced her. She pulled away from me, and when she looked at me, I saw she was crying.

"Why, Victor? Why didn't you tell me?"

"Tell you? Anna, I don't think I understand. Tell you what?"

She seemed to be able to tell by the sincerity and concern in my eyes that I wasn't playing petty mind games with her.

"You truly do not know?" she asked.

I shook my head.

"Oh God," she whispered, putting her hand to her lips and turning away.

She went into the drawer of her nightstand and held out a book. "You mean to tell me you never saw this?"

I took it from her hands, not responding. My eyes were glued to it. I couldn't move. I sat down on the bed and opened the book.

"Oh my God, Anna," I whispered so quietly I barely heard myself. "How…?"

The book she had given me was Daniel's journal—my master's diary.

November 8, 1785

The air is cool tonight, and I enjoy it. I wonder if Victor has even noticed my love for Anna. I love her, though I don't think I would ever tell him that. The child drives me mad; she seems to believe that everything Victor and I must do is for her. I didn't want her to be one of us; I knew it would be wrong.

She clung to me last night, asking me strange questions.

"Father," she whimpered, clinging to the skirt of my coat, "why do you push me away?"

"Leave me alone," I said. "You're pestering me again."

I pulled away, and she fell to her knees.

"Father!" she called. "Why don't you love me anymore? Why are you mean, Father? Why don't you care for Victor anymore? Why won't you ever speak to me about things?"

She began screaming as I continued walking away. "Father!" She stood to her feet and quickened her pace, following every move I made.

"Why, Father?" She was terribly angry. "Why don't you ever tell me how I came to be a vampire?"

"What are you talking about, Anna? You've always been this way."

"That's what I thought until I realize I used to have a family, and I see how you call us vampires, but you call the outsiders mortals. Why are we different, Father? Tell me!"

"I don't know!" I yelled, turning to her, startling her. "All right? I don't know these things, Anna. Why should I? Do you think I know everything? Don't ask me questions. They don't matter. What matters is what is—all right? Now stop pestering me!"

Her eyes filled with tears, and she stormed out of the room. I sighed and fell back in the chair behind me and put my hand to my forehead.

That morning came a very terrible dream. I know it may sound crazy, but I dreamed about my captors—about the night when Eric and Thaddeus had made me and when Ashman had found me. I remembered the teachings of Ashman, but also I remember that we left for a group. He said a strange name, something about how they needed him as their Cassiodorus, as their religious leader, and that I was taught all I needed to know.

Ashman took care of me after my makers left me. They knew little and cared even less. I miss Ashman, and to this day, I wonder where he is, this ancient vampire, the first heir to The Father. I wonder still! The dream, I suppose, wasn't terrible, for the presence of Ashman had comforted me, and I enjoyed feeling close to him again. The dream made those memories fresher in my mind, and I would like to share these things with Victor, but I can't. I am not yet ready to speak of them. I don't want him to call me a coward. I am not a coward. I will not weep in his presence. I must be strong for him. I must be powerful for him. I must be the master that he needs. I love him so much. I only wanted to help him in the first place. I want him to be happy.

November 9, 1785

I ignored Anna again today, but she ignored me too. I wish I could answer her questions. I wish I could tell her what it was like being human, what it was like being in love and having a life, but I can't. She clings to Victor every moment, and as much as it hurts me, I don't let them know I love her. I am not included in their love, and that's all right. They have their fun dancing and singing as though life were one big Shakespearean play, but it isn't, and it drives me mad. My very own child feels bitter toward me, and Anna would probably destroy me if she could—get rid of me so she could be with Victor and do what she pleased with Victor without my constant rules pressing upon her every second.

I love the child as I have confessed, but I don't want her around any longer. She hates me, and I can't bear that. I can't bear the way Victor looks at me, the way his eyes don't hold the same love that they used to for me. I want to leave him, to let him have his life with Anna, and when he is ready to let that go, I will bring him back to me. I can't bring myself to leave him yet. I love him too much.

I know I must leave soon, of course, before Anna's mind powers develop anymore. I fear that my thoughts will be read when I am not aware of her presence. I can't let her know what I did. Hatred will be her only thoughts when she finds out what I did to her family. She is Anna Foster, though Victor doesn't even know that. I destroyed the rest of the family, but I couldn't bring myself to destroy Anna. She was too beautiful. I couldn't take her in my arms and let her die. I just couldn't do it. I couldn't tell this to Victor no matter what. I have to be strong for him. Otherwise, he may make the same mistakes that I have made. I have regrets for killing her family, and I intended on redeeming myself from that guilt by taking care of her and loving her as she deserved, but that opportunity was given to Victor instead. After all, hadn't I given her to Victor? He painted flowers on her walls, cleans up after her, brings her gifts from stores that he takes from his victims, speaks to her and answers her questions about the world of love. They are dreamers, and she will lead Victor astray on a path of wild dreams where he will forget what he is and make horrible mistakes. I can't watch that happen to him. I love him too much!

. . .

As I read these things, I realized that Daniel was not the heartless creature I once imagined him to be. Everything he did was for me, and he did still love us. But the pain overpowered the joy, and Anna confronted me as I sat on my bed, weeping bitterly into my hands.

"It's all right, Father," she whispered. "I already knew. I have known for a long time, Victor. I am sorry that I yelled at you."

"Please tell me you love me, Anna."

"I love you. Truly I do." She touched my shoulder and left the room.

I cried for a long time. I was ashamed to cry, but the tears were real and could not be held back.

I couldn't hate Daniel for this, could I? After what I had done to the Cornallys, that wouldn't be fair. I couldn't hate him, and I still don't.

November 11, 1785

I can't say I intended on staying with Victor after I made him. I can't say I meant to return that night when he was alone. But I had fallen in love with him. I hadn't meant to, but I did. I knew his soul, and I loved it—as mortal and immortal. So, I came back to him and never let on that I had other intentions. Creating and walking away was all I was taught. My makers knew nothing, nor did they care, at least not about anything but their power. They left me an orphan. All I do when I'm alone is remember that night when I was taken to the home of these men. It was a dark house with golden sheets on the beds and chandeliers hanging from the ceiling of every room. I was awakened by the sound of their voices, and when I opened my eyes, I knew at once that I was a long way from home and all the people out looking for me would never find me. My father was a nobleman by nature, but he never seemed to care much about me. Perhaps he wasn't looking for me; perhaps he didn't care if I ever returned.

I can remember staring petrified at the creatures that leaned over me. They smiled when they realized how frightened I was. I don't remember what they had said to me or even if they spoke at all. All I remember is that both of them had dark, cruel eyes and jet-black hair. Of course, I realized that they weren't human, but at the time, that was the least of my fears.

The next memory is of the night when a soft voice awoke me. I looked at the man who spoke to me, who kissed the tears off my cheeks with his warm, soft lips, who savored the taste of my blood as I wept in his arms. My Ashman—the ancient accursed Pharaoh of Egypt whose entire bloodline was erased from history. My Ashman, who took me in and taught me the ways of our kind. My master, my father...my Ashman. I weep now as I write this; I hope I can conceal my tears from Victor. As I had said before...I MUST be strong for him. For Anna too.

I couldn't help but feel intense hatred toward Daniel for what he had done to Anna. He had brought so much pain to her, the same pain I had taken murderess revenge for. I wanted to hate him. I wanted to never miss him again. I knew, however, that could never be.

Anna came in again as I tried to hide the pain in my eyes, closing off my mind.

"You do not need to hide from me," she said, placing a soft hand on my cheek. "I do not suffer, my love. I don't lie awake and cry. I don't call out for my mother in my dreams. I am unsure why. Maybe I should—but I don't. I have you. You have always taken care of me. I love you more than anything."

She embraced me in a way she never had before. She held tightly, as if afraid to let me go. I could feel the emotion in her radiating through me.

The months passed as I searched for another of our kind to no avail. There was one way I thought to find the one Daniel had written about. I left letters on the streets after dark where few mortals would be. Obviously, he had found them as I knew he would have. He probably sensed I was here the moment I arrived.

The letters said my name was Victor Miller and that from the child of Ashman The Great, I was given his name; in return for his teachings and guidance, I would do whatever he wished.

I slept restlessly one morning beside Anna and was aroused in the dark by the sound of a beating heart and a tremble in the earth. I thought I had been dreaming, but when I heard Anna whisper my name, I was sure I was awake, and something was going on.

His name came to my mind from his, but I wasn't yet sure if it was real. I felt him grasp my arm and lift me from my bed.

"Drink, young one," I heard him say, his voice ringing with age like silver bells.

I felt the heat of his flesh against my mouth and the fire of his blood through my body.

When it was over, I whispered the only word I could. "Relone?"

And I heard his quiet yet definite response. "Yes."

Chapter Nine

VICTOR PAUSED.

"Is there more?"

"Of course," he answered. "There is much more. I did not stay with Relone for long. There were too many things I needed to learn that Relone could not offer me. I knew I needed to find his maker. The one called The King. Verarsoe. At the time, I could not be sure he was even real, but I will get to that. You will know everything, Will...in time."

I suddenly remembered my little Anna, and I extended my arm to feel for her. She grasped my hand, and instantly I felt comfort wash over me. The power of this creature frightened me deeply. I could feel his strength emanating from him—shaking the atmosphere of the earth! I didn't want him to leave, as much as I might have wished it in my mind. I had looked for him, and he had found me. I couldn't speak yet, but I don't think he wanted me to.

"I knew you were here the very day you arrived—Victor

Miller," he whispered. "I could feel you, and I received every letter."

I couldn't respond yet. I quite suddenly became aware that perhaps this was not the best thing for us. This creature had a lot more power than Daniel, and I feared too much power…well…corrupts. I tried not to let this feeling be seen.

"I want you to meet me somewhere," he said. "Tomorrow evening, there is something I must show you. Meet me at the street corner near the bookstore."

Before I could respond, he was gone. Anna and I didn't speak a word about him until the next evening.

"I'm afraid of him, Father. What if he's mean like Daniel was?"

"I am horrified to say, my love…that I don't know."

"I don't think I wish to come with you. I want to stay here."

I was mildly *confused* at first, but it soon transformed. I felt hurt she didn't want to be with me for something so important.

"You may stay," I told her, trying not to show the pain. I wanted Anna with me always, and to know that she didn't want to come along with me, that she didn't believe in my judgment—it broke my heart in many ways.

"I won't do it if it hurts you," she said, climbing up on my lap. "I won't do anything that hurts you." She kissed me and whispered something, but I don't remember what she said. "I'll come with you, Victor. All right?"

"Yes, Anna. It's good."

"I know when things hurt you. You can't hide that from me, my love."

I smiled thinly. "I should have known. Come now. Get your coat."

We left to the street corner near the bookstore and waited for Relone. Before I had even seen a shadow of him, I could feel that tremor in the atmosphere, and Anna was the only one standing beside me. I had to hold her up, but there was nobody to hold me up, and I stumbled. My legs shook like water from my fear.

He approached slowly, moving as though his feet weren't touching the ground. I studied the way the light danced upon his gray hair. I knew he couldn't have been much older than me when he was made.

"I am glad to know you came," he said to me softly.

His voice made me shudder. "You told me to."

He smiled, and the beauty of him startled me.

"There is something you must see. Come now—please."

I let him lead Anna and me to a catacomb where he spent his time. The place was beautiful. Relone must have been a lover of light. There were torches along the walls, and as I stared at the flames, I grew nervous, remembering it was the only thing besides the sun that could really hurt me.

There were books everywhere as if he was some kind of scholar in his mortal years. The works of Aristotle and Plato were packed on shelves and strewn across a redwood desk.

Relone made himself comfortable in a floral upholstered chair and gave me a very thin, false smile. "Sit."

I shook my head and tightened my grip on Anna's hand. "What do you want?"

He chuckled. "What do I want? It's you who was seeking me. Don't you remember, Victor Miller?"

"Yes. But in exchange for your teachings—what do you want?"

"You should not feel ashamed," he answered kindly, shaking his head.

"Who says I am ashamed?"

He smiled again. "You did. Only not in so many words." His voice was soft. He almost seemed to care for me in some way already. "I have taken in many vampires who were left by their makers. They all eventually leave, of course, but for now, I have three lovely companions that I like to call my brides."

I realized then that I did feel the presence of others. I had been so distracted by Relone's power I was not aware of them.

"Were they—?"

"Yes," he answered. "They were abandoned as you were, and I saved them, as I am going to save you, but you must tell me—what are you willing to give me? Are you willing to save me?"

"What are you asking?"

He chuckled again.

It felt synthetic almost, but all the same, it made me shudder.

He sighed and slouched down in his chair. "If I am to guide you, perhaps you could guide me."

"Guide *you*?"

"Into this age. To lead me through this century."

I wasn't sure what he meant, and for a moment, I had forgotten entirely about Anna. I hadn't realized she was no longer standing beside me.

"What do you want?" I asked again.

"Nothing. Just you."

"Me?"

Relone subtly nodded. "Yes. I want you, Victor, as a companion, one who will not leave me after I have taught you all you desire to know. I am beginning to sink into emptiness. Without you, I am unsure what's left."

"I'm not sure I understand."

"I want you as my child, Victor. Isn't that what you had wanted in the first place?"

Anna said my name, making me aware of her presence. She hadn't been standing beside me the whole time, but I didn't know where she had been.

"Come. Please, Father, let's go home."

I looked into her pleading blue eyes, gave Relone a smile that promised my return, and left.

She sighed, pacing through the room as Daniel used to do.

"What is it?" I asked.

She halted then. "What?"

"What is it that's troubling you?"

"It's nothing." She paused, seeming to consider her words. "I fear Relone, Father. I have this feeling he wants to hurt me."

"Hurt you?" I yelled. "Why would you think such a thing, Anna?"

"I don't know. He wants you, but I do not think he wants me, and if he does, I am sorry to say, Father—that I don't want him."

"Why do you say that?"

"I don't want a vampire old and strong like Relone. In comparison to Relone, I am beginning to want Daniel back."

"Don't do this, Anna. I will not deny I want Daniel back, that I never wanted him to leave in the first place. But he is gone now, my love. Who else is there?"

She sighed. "I guess there is nobody else for you, is there?"

I shook my head. "Everything is going to be fine."

"I admire your faith, Father…as I always have."

She embraced me, and I savored the feel of her in my arms. She left the room, but I could still feel her apprehension in my bones.

I sighed and sat on my bed, pondering the decision I would be forced to make. I needed Relone, but was it really what would make me happy? After all, I seemed to be doing well on my own.

I believe now that it was my loneliness that made me want Relone, more than anything. Even with Anna, there was something missing—some hole that Daniel had left, a void I needed desperately to fill. I was entranced and infatuated with his power. I had always been one that thirsted for knowledge, and knowledge was something he had much of.

Daniel had told me that my love for knowledge was what convinced him to choose me; perhaps that's what Relone liked about me as well.

I met him again a few evenings later, and there he was—waiting for me.

"Why me?" I asked soberly, almost passively.

"What do you mean?"

"Why, out of all, do you have this desire for me to be your child, Relone?"

"Can't you see that it takes but one look to fall in love with you, Victor?" He chuckled.

"But why? Is this what you are asking in return? An apprentice that will become your eternal companion?"

"It is."

"An eternity with you in exchange for years of teachings?"

He sighed. "Maybe not forever. Forever is an awfully long time, don't you think, Victor?"

I nodded.

"Just admit you want me as your master. Just admit that you have a sense of love for the knowledge I possess."

"I never denied that, Relone. Even Anna sees it in my eyes."

"Then why do you hold back from me, Victor? Why do you refuse to look at me sometimes?"

"I hate the desire I have for your knowledge. If I come to you, I will never be free of you."

He chuckled. "You can't refuse me, can you?"

I sighed. "I can, Relone. I don't want to like you."

"But you do."

"No," I whispered, "but if I come to you and let you teach me—I will."

He smiled.

"What about the vampires you have chosen?"

"They don't have what I need. You can guide me into the new era, can't you?"

"I do not desire to. I wish to remain out of touch with all things. I wish not to reflect my era."

I saw a sudden look of anguish on his face, and I put my hand on his shoulder, feeling the inhuman hardness of his flesh.

"This is not for me. I only wish to stay here with my

child and remain the same Victor Miller I have always been."

"Your child?"

"Yes," I answered. "Anna—"

"I know of whom you speak."

"She is my child."

"And do you honestly think that she will want you forever?" He was smiling, and it confused me but made me want to be enfolded in his arms.

"What are you saying?" I snapped. I think he felt the terror in my voice.

"You have found your new companion. Will she find hers?"

I didn't respond.

"You will leave her for me."

"That could never happen."

"And yet your affection toward her is waning."

I tried to remember the last time I had touched Anna in a loving way. Wasn't it just last night I had held her? "Anna is my daughter. She is my life."

"Look at her."

I turned my gaze toward a black-haired woman, realizing again that Anna wasn't standing at my side. There were three beautiful women surrounding Anna like a pack of wolves. They tousled her auburn hair and made her laugh. They spoke to her silently, but I couldn't read their thoughts. I watched as Anna climbed upon the lap of the woman known as Monique. She wrapped her arms around her neck as she had done with me years ago. I instantly stood to my feet without meaning to.

"Come now, Anna. We're going home."

"But we've just arrived," she argued, clinging to Monique.

"Come, Anna. Come on now."

She sighed and tightened her grip on the woman as to embrace her.

Anna slid off her companion's lap, and I extended my arm behind my back. She took my hand, and with one more look into Relone's eyes, I lifted Anna into my arms and carried her home, thinking as I did that I would never leave her.

I could feel stiffening in my arms before we reached the door. I set her down, and she walked ahead of me into the house without even a glance. I could feel I was losing her.

Chapter Ten

A FEW WEEKS LATER, I met with Relone again. Anna stayed at the hotel as I had kindly asked of her.

"You cannot make me leave her," I told him desperately.

"Come to Boston with me," he said as if he heard nothing I had just told him. His emotion was hidden from me; I wasn't sure exactly what he was feeling at the moment.

"Boston?" I questioned. "Why Boston?"

"It's a place where many of our kind dwell—including my maker."

"Your maker?"

"I left him years ago," he started. It was as if he were in some dramatic play and had a sad, heartfelt speech memorized. "I left to Boston. Being the person that he was, he eventually came back for me. Years later, I longed for my home. I came back to France, but my maker remained in Boston with a coven he calls Satan's Own, where he remains to this day."

I couldn't respond. I took a breath and leaned back in the chair. "There are others there?"

"Yes. Many others."

Thoughts rushed through my mind; there were others like me. Perhaps if Anna knew this, she would decide to trust him.

"Perhaps," Relone replied.

I gasped, sinking down in my chair, not realizing my thoughts could be read so easily. His emotions were even more veiled than they were before—veiled by smiles and synthetic looks of content. Something was bothering him.

"Perhaps," he repeated. "But perhaps not, for Anna was young when she was made. There are elders who wouldn't hear of it. It's a sin to create one who will need you forever, somebody who is unable to leave you and take care of herself."

"So what do I do?" I asked. "There are others like me out there—others who can teach me things, show me things. For once I won't be forced to hide away. For once I won't have to be alone. I want to stay with you, Relone, but if you do not wish to keep Anna, you cannot keep me."

"And why is that?" I heard a voice from behind me.

I turned to see Anna dressed in a pretty red gown, her hair piled in curls upon her head, her eyes slightly filled with tears.

"Anna!" I yelled. "Why are you here?"

"Why are *you*?" she whispered.

"Anna—"

"I mean it, Victor. Tell me why. Tell me why you can't keep Relone."

"Because I want to keep you. Because I am okay with you staying with me forever. Because I do not fear the elders. Because you are my daughter. I love you, Anna."

She didn't answer immediately; I knew she was going to cry. "I want you to go with him. I will be all right, but you need Relone."

"No. Anna, you don't understand. If I have you, I am happy."

She shook her head. "You need him. I can see it."

"I need you too."

"You can't leave me because I happen to be the one that links you to Daniel. I happen to be the one that reminds you that he will return someday. Listen to me, my love—keep Relone. Let him teach you. I cannot be here any longer."

"You don't mean that. Please, Anna. You said you would never leave me."

"I want you to have Relone. Do this for me, Father—please!"

"Anna," I whispered quietly. "Please tell me you love me. Please tell me you are not doing this because you do not love me anymore."

"I will always love you, Father. When Daniel comes back…you know where to find me. When at last you have let go of your mortal grief—just come find me."

I saw Monique emerge from another part of the catacomb and grasp my Anna's hand. My daughter buried her face in the woman's chest and then I heard it—the miserable sound that I had never before heard Anna make—she was crying. I felt as if I needed to cover my ears before the sound swallowed me up and destroyed me. I began softly caressing her shoulder and wrapping my fingers around her curls of reddened hair. Her tears made me weep as well. She turned to me and without warning leapt into my arms and embraced me tighter than she ever had before, gripping my shirt with her fingernails. I couldn't tell if she was going to let go or not, but I didn't want her to. Her arms were as strong as metal clamps, but she was still warm and tender.

"Please don't forget how to love me, Father," she whispered through her tears. "My Victor, my love."

"I will love you until the day I die."

"When eternity ends?"

"And beyond. This is not truly goodbye, my love—I will see you again."

She smiled. "Goodbye, Victor."

"Goodbye, my Anna."

I looked at Relone, and he nodded.

"I love her," I said.

"I understand. She is your daughter."

My love for Anna was more than that, but I didn't correct him.

This is what Anna wanted, what she needed, what she had always needed—a mother.

Relone said we were going to Boston.

"To the ship then," I said.

After we boarded the ship, I stood upon the deck, watching the dark water below. I heard Relone approach.

"Is this a curse?" I asked. "Was I cursed with this life?"

"Do you think it a curse? Do you think it so vile and evil?"

"I don't know. The world itself seems against me, and the more days that pass, the more miserable I grow."

"Perhaps you need a child of your own."

"No. I do not wish to turn another. I have you now."

"Is that all you need?"

I sighed, realizing that without Anna, Relone was just not enough. I knew deep down he and I would not stay together for long. I was just not ready to move on. I needed to be alone with my suffering before putting it behind me.

Chapter Eleven

RELONE and I stayed together on the ship, and all the while, I contemplated whether or not it really was a good idea going to Boston. It is true that most vampires don't like each other, but the need for the company and sometimes companionship of their own kind is greatly needed. Some immortals perish after being alone so long. That's what I feared for myself and for Relone as well.

I lay in bed that morning, realizing I could hear the mortal voices and thoughts on the ship. I grew to enjoy these sounds; I could choose which ones to listen to and which ones to ignore. I grew to admire a woman by the name of Hannah; she had golden hair and deep, dark eyes. She had been widowed and was moving to Boston for reasons that her mind had hidden from me. The fascination with her soon grew to infatuation. She was miserable as I was miserable. I fell in love with her as it were and even mourned when I learned she had fallen terribly ill. I had an almost painful longing to save her as I knew I could, but I also knew she would only find peace if she were to die and be reunited with her beloved husband. And so I did nothing.

The pain I felt was crippling, but I chose to keep it as my own. My mortal emotions were all that kept me who I was, and I didn't want to change.

As the days grew dull without Hannah, I had found another mortal who in a way had touched the mortal heart I still possessed somewhere inside me. Adam was his name. He was a beautiful boy with so much love inside him. He was just married a few years ago and was blessed with an absolutely gorgeous, golden-haired daughter. She reminded me of Anna. She was so tender toward Adam and her mother, Mary, as well. There was so much confusion in her little angelic eyes, not understanding where they were going or why. I grew to adore this family as I watched them. I felt very close to them. I wanted to speak to them, to share in their love. I used to laugh at the way Adam would dance with his daughter on the deck of the ship. I loved them truly. They were the family that families dream of being part of.

I wish I could have said that Adam was happy, but in truth—he was not. He was also miserable, which is what drew me to him. He was forced from his beautiful home in Geneva Switzerland by the will of his wife, the wish that he could not deny her. He was sad to leave his home, all that he had known, the place he had grown up, the place he had gone to school and met Mary, the place that his child, Madeline, was born, but after the French invasion, he knew there was no other choice.

As I grew to love this family, I prepared myself to meet them. Though, of course, I knew it was my job to remain in the shadows. I couldn't stand not being able to share in their love and comfort Adam from the loss of his home. Before I had been given the chance to introduce myself, I was alarmed by the shattering cries of my darling Adam and his wife. A horrible misfortune had occurred. Adam's beloved daughter had been struck with a severe case of Scarlet Fever. He wept and screamed for her. I saw his pain as he began to lose his sanity, flinging open the windows and cursing at God.

I couldn't stand to watch him any longer. I wept with him, and once more, Relone had given me the speech about what separates us from mortals, but again—I didn't give it much thought. This boy was going to lose his daughter, and there was nothing he could do to stop it. I knew the pain he was suffering, the pain of losing a daughter, and that's when it hit me. I could save her. I could help him to help her. I could make it so he never had to lose her. Couldn't I? I smiled at these thoughts.

I spoke to Relone about my undefeatable love for Adam and his family.

"I must, Relone," I said. "Don't you see? I could be the reason his daughter lives. Her fate is in my hands. I can save her life!"

"But should you?"

"Why should I not?" I snapped. "Please don't do this to me, Relone. Tell me I can do this. Tell me it's a good decision."

"You don't need me to tell you that, Victor."

"She's so innocent."

"It could be a ghastly mistake," he started. "Don't you remember what I had said? It's forbidden to make one as young as her."

I sighed. "I know, but why should he go through the

same pain I went through when I can spare him that? She's dying, Relone—dying, and she's only so young."

Relone sighed and lifted his hands as if he were angry—but he was smiling. "You are a stubborn one. There is no way to convince you otherwise."

I found Adam a couple of nights later while he stood upon the deck, listening to the water below, thinking of his sick baby girl facing the hands of death growing closer and closer each second that passed. I whispered his name, and with a startled gasp, he spun around. I laughed and quickened my movement.

He ran from me, panicked. I decided to have fun with this. I whispered his name again.

I stopped before him and stared at him tensely.

"Who are you?" he demanded.

I laughed, making sure my lips didn't move, and stepped closer until Adam's fear drove him to a panicking sprint.

"Leave me, you devil!" I heard him call out as he ran.

I chased him effortlessly, and with one quick grasp of my arms, I had him close to me with my teeth pressed to his throat, waiting for the bite. His blue eyes grew big and tear filled, his fear overflowing his soul, but I didn't want him to be afraid anymore. I tried to rise from the deck, but I couldn't. I could smell blood. I could taste it. I wanted it! I had to have it! I bit hard into the soft flesh of his neck. I couldn't stop; the ecstasy let me rise from the ground as I took his life into my own. His blood flowed with pain and grief, mingled with his terror. I could taste it all—everything! I realized suddenly that the strikingly gorgeous young man in my arms was dying, that I was drinking too much. But I couldn't stop.

I begged myself to pull back, to release him before I

killed him. I eventually forced my mouth from the wound on his neck and lowered him gently to the ground where he struggled for air.

Oh, Adam, I thought. *Oh God—I'm sorry!*

He begged me to help him.

"I know what you need," I said, "and I can give it to you."

"Help me," he forced out. I could hear the pain in his voice.

"You know what you need, my young friend," I whispered in his ear. "Tell me you want it."

I heard him struggle out the response. "Yes…I want it."

I bit my wrist and pressed it to his lips. I could feel the pressure of his mouth as he drank. I felt his muscles tighten and grasp my wrist with his hands as if the pleasure of it was too much to let go. I tried to pull away, but he wouldn't stop. He continued to drink, and I didn't want to force myself from him for fear of hurting him.

I felt as if he had broken the very circuit of my life. I didn't want to hurt him, but I couldn't wait any longer. I pulled away from him, weakened and in agony.

"Please," I heard him beg. "Don't let the pain come back."

"It needs to happen. You are giving up all that is human. All of your mortal qualities are leaving your body. Don't fight the changes, or it will be even more painful!"

I watched as his skin turned whiter, and his eyes grew tense. I watched as my power gave him all that he was receiving. I watched as the fangs grew in his mouth, and suddenly his pain was gone. He tried to speak, but no words came out.

"You're welcome," I said to him kindly.

I told him to look around with his newly gained eyes, and he stared as if in fascination of everything around him.

"My name," I started as kindly as I knew how, "is Victor Miller."

He smiled at me, and it charmed me for a moment. I reached into the inside pocket of my jacket and handed him a mirror. He looked in horror, the way I had over forty years ago.

He brushed the strands of his dark hair from his eyes and touched his face with his fingertips. "What have you done to me?"

I told him that he had the knowledge of what he was, that he had the knowledge of how he had to live and feed. I had released that into him through my gifted blood.

He met me the next night as I had told him to. I explained everything I could. I mentioned I knew about his daughter, but he refused to curse her. He said he could not take away her innocence.

He exploded with rage, yelling out to me, calling me names. "Evil stalker of the night," "fiend," "monster."

I became frightened, realizing it may be that I had brought him into my world for a purpose that would never be fulfilled, that this creation had been done in vain. "Do it!" I told him. "Do it…or I will."

"Why are you doing this to me?"

I told him it was because he needed me to. It was because if he didn't, then his daughter would die, and he would never forgive himself. It took him long moments to finally decide deep within his mind that this was what he wanted, that saving Madeline's life was truly all he ever wanted in the first place.

"I must say," I started, "this ship takes less time than I

expected. By the time we reach Boston, you will be without me."

"Without you?" he yelled. "How can I be without you? You are my maker. I—"

"Don't say it, Adam!" I yelled. "Do not say that you love me!"

I knew his mind and his heart, and I knew there may come a time when he feels hatred toward the dark gift and would blame me for his misery, for who else could there possibly be to blame? He was very strong, stronger than I ever could have imagined. I had to block my mind because he had the gift.

It was strange the way he looked at me, the way he wept from the guilt of what he had to do. He hated what I had done to him; he spoke of how it was ghastly and evil, terrible and accursed. I said nothing about how it was beautiful or magical, nothing about how it was wonderful or amazing.

The nights went by slowly after that. Relone asked me if I was sure that I had not made a mistake. He told me Adam's daughter was a lot stronger than I realized she would be, stronger than Adam.

He told me that, of course, Adam would make his wife, as I already knew. He said that she would become a monster, killing ruthlessly without care or secret.

"A vampire is what she would have been, but evil is what she would have become. It's her or our race."

I didn't know what to say at first. "So what do we do?"

"Leave that to me."

The night I heard the cries of Adam and Madeline in my head, I knew what Relone had done. Their wailing was hard to stand, and eventually, it brought me to tears. Relone returned, and instantly I dried my eyes and pushed past the grief. Victor Miller doesn't weep; Victor Miller is not a coward.

"I don't think you're a coward," he said.

"Stop reading my thoughts! I cannot read yours."

"You don't know how strong you are, do you, Victor Miller?"

"Of course I do."

He smiled. "Stronger than I was at your age."

"Am I?"

"A lot. Use it for good."

"Do you think that God hates us for what we do?"

"I wish I could say something other than the fact that I don't know. Many have asked that question, and none have been given an answer."

"Is there nobody that knows?" I asked desperately.

"Find another someday, one older than me. Perhaps he could answer your questions."

"What did you do?" I asked sadly.

"You don't want me to tell you that," he responded, "for even I am saddened by it."

"I won't be sad. You said it yourself—I am stronger than I even know."

He paused for a moment. "Mary is dead."

I knew before he said it, and yet I still felt anger build inside me. I tried to push it down, bury it before I attacked Relone.

"You are sad?"

"No, of course not." I stood up and turned away as to hide my grief. "I would have done it too."

I wasn't sure if he believed me, and at the time, I didn't

care. We would be in Boston soon, and I really hoped I could be all right. Hoped Adam could be all right too. I had no conception of what I had done to him, did I?

So many ghastly and wonderful things followed the next years with and without Relone, and here is where the true story begins. The ship had docked; the time…had come.

Chapter Twelve

AS SOON AS we arrived in Boston, it took all my self-control to stay away from Adam. I wanted to go to him, to comfort him from the loss of his wife. I wanted to be near him more than anything. I knew it could not be. Not yet. I could not be the master he needed at the time, and I was not ready to part with Relone.

Relone and I rented a hotel room for a few nights. I sat down in a chair opposite him and stared, waiting for what I wanted him to tell me.

"My maker may be able to give you the answers you desire, the reason you are here."

"Who is he?"

"The King," he answered, leaning forward, eyes big and filled with hidden pain. "The first heir of The Father."

"The Father?"

"The first of our kind. Verarsoe, or The King as he is often referred to, was the first of his children. Perhaps he may have some answers that I still do not. Remember, Victor, he is older than I am, a teacher that I can never be, but if you wish to stay as his child as I honestly fear you will, I believe that one of these days, he will hurt you the way he hurt me."

"What do you mean?"

"He can be cruel, Victor," he said solemnly, not making eye contact with me. "He can be mean."

"I know. I could have guessed that about a creature such as him. I'm prepared for it, Relone."

"So you want him to be your master?"

"I...don't know." I paused for a moment. "Yes...I think I do."

"Promise me you will be careful, Victor. I don't want you to get hurt."

I nodded. I knew I needed Verarsoe, as all children do. So many have looked for him and died trying. The King hates being followed, and yes, he knows when somebody is looking for him. If he believes one to not be worthy of his teachings, he will not hesitate to destroy them.

I wasn't afraid. Relone had sent me, and as much as he may say otherwise, Verarsoe loved Relone. We all love our children.

Relone and I said a long and warm farewell, and I set off for The King.

I cried for days over Anna, and occasionally, I would slip my hand into my jacket pocket and fall into panic realizing my piano key wasn't there. But then I remembered Anna, and I twisted my fingers around the ribbon she had given me in exchange for my piano key, feeling her presence until the pain consumed me and I needed peace. I knew peace only when I killed. I stopped at hotels, graves, and abandoned sheds. I never had one true home, and I still don't.

I walked the streets, waiting for the perfect victim to

cross my path. There was a child; she had deep auburn hair and enormous blue eyes. Anna. Of course, it wasn't Anna, but she looked like her, felt like her, gave me that slow, passive look like her. I found I wanted her. I can clearly remember whispering the name as she walked past me, holding tightly to her mother's hand. The child kept her eyes on me, staring at me over her shoulder. Her blood would give me peace, but I couldn't kill her. That would not be possible. She was too innocent, too sweet, and too tender. She was not the perfect victim I was waiting for that night, and I cannot recall feeding at all before I was concealed beneath the warm blankets of my bed as the sun rose high.

As I lay there in that uncomfortable hotel bed, waiting to sleep, I asked myself, why am I here? I asked myself that question continuously. Why am I an immortal superhuman? Why did God create us to destroy his children? I was raised to trust in God. He was all I ever had, but suddenly, God began to fade from my life. All the things I used to know had been stripped away. Now I was alone without a family, a religion, or a life.

I needed some answers. I needed some love. I needed… Verarsoe. "Knowledge, answers, and reason are what he could give to me," I whispered to myself as tears forced their way to my eyes.

"My God, Daniel—what have you done to me?" My voice faded to a whisper. "What have you done to me?" I covered my face with my hands and wept.

Yes, I love the dark gift, but I also hate being alone. I hate the way the world changes around me and new lifestyles and worldviews spring up unexpectedly as I remain Victor Miller as I have always been.

My search for Verarsoe started simply enough. I stopped at every hotel and bed and breakfast I could find, searching for a single sign of one of our kind, but I found nothing. For all I knew at the time, this king that Relone spoke of could easily be nothing more than a made-up legend. I told myself over and over that Verarsoe was real and that if I didn't find him, he would find me.

I found a grave to sleep in that night. I awoke tired in the dark to a shaking in the ground, like the power of an immortal—power that was emanating from its soul the same way it had emanated from Relone. Before I realized what I was doing, I found myself clawing my way to the surface, tasting the fresh dirt in my mouth, feeling it clinging to my hair. I was frantic to get out, frantic to find the owner of that heartbeat that throbbed in my head. I gripped the outer ground with my fingernails and pulled myself out with a mortal reaction of gasping for the air I didn't need.

"Shh," I heard a voice say. "Do not be afraid. I know who you are, and I'm not going to hurt you."

I didn't respond. I just watched the eyes before me gathering the light. The glow startled me, but what startled me more was the thought that my eyes must have been glowing as well. I stood to my feet, shaking so furiously I could barely keep my balance. I reached out and touched the creature's hand. I could feel eons of life flowing through him, filling my body with an unnatural weakness. The incredible age in him weakened and confused me to where I was practically dizzy. I stared without blinking. His hair was black and wavy, held back with a dark-colored ribbon. The eyes were of the darkest brown, though it was hard to tell through the glow. He looked like glass almost. I couldn't believe he was alive, and I don't know how anybody else could. I felt the blood sweat forming on my face; it was the most pathetic, disgusting feeling I had ever had—the feeling of weakness and fear. I removed my fingers from his hand and let my head spin.

"Relone…" I whispered as the only word I was able to force out.

The creature smiled, and it frightened me. "Yes," he said. "Relone told me about you. You're growing older and stronger, Victor Miller. If you do not find a companion, somebody to share a life with, you are going to spend eternity as a mindless predator. I think it would be better for you not to die."

"I don't want to die," I answered.

"Nobody does," he whispered softly. "Are you going to let me save you?"

I couldn't answer. I couldn't move. I was too weak and confused.

"I can teach you things."

I moved toward him, and without even thinking, I embraced him, wrapping my arms around his ribs as if I knew him. I held on and let his power flow through me. I am unsure why I held so steadily without loosening my grip. Perhaps it was a feeling of love that he brought out of me, like a feeling of tenderness and humanity that I had long since lost, the feeling that made me want to be held in his arms. I felt him return my embrace. How warm and alive he felt against me, yet how strong and unnatural he felt at the same time.

My eyes welled with tears as a feeling of sadness came to me, a feeling I hadn't felt since the night my family died. I was feeling this creature's emotions, the emotions he had experienced in all his eons of life. I wanted to feel more, to feel all of his pain and joy at once even if it would destroy me.

"Drink, my young one," he whispered.

I held tighter.

"Victor…"

I held him with all my strength, but he pushed me forward with no more than an ounce of his own.

"Drink, my child."

I watched him lift his wrist, and I followed it with my eyes. He revealed his beautiful, broadly built chest and gashed it with his nails. It startled me, but the bleeding wound only added to the pure perfection of his body, and I wished I could have told him that. He pressed me toward him, and I locked myself on the wound, drinking and biting, widening the opening with my teeth as I drank and drank and drank. It didn't taste like blood; it tasted like liquid metal and fire. Pure and natural—meant for me. When at last I pulled away, I fell weak against him. I could feel the blood staining my hair as I leaned my head upon his chest.

"Don't worry," he whispered. "You are weak because you are confused. I have released power into you, Victor Miller, power that you need, so do not be afraid. When you awake, you will feel stronger than you ever have before, and then I can answer your questions."

I did sleep, and I don't know how long. I was unaware of whether it was day or night the moment I fell softly into Verarsoe's arms, and I don't know how late it was when I fell asleep in them, but when I awoke, it was evening.

"Open your gentle eyes, Victor," I heard him say.

I opened my eyes and saw him smiling before me.

"There is so much you desire to know, Victor, and I can teach you."

I smiled and sat up. At last I had found him, a teacher that neither Daniel nor Relone could have ever been.

For the first time now, I found myself looking around examining the place he had taken me. It was almost identical to Relone's catacomb. I understood then. Verarsoe really was Relone's maker, and I was very sure Relone had missed his home so had built his own. He was in Boston somewhere now, no doubt building another.

There were chairs and lamps everywhere. The King must have been a true lover of light. I realized I had awakened in a bed much too large for myself. It was then my eyes could really see The King. He was at least half a foot taller than me.

The ceiling appeared to be almost ten feet above my head. I smiled as I gazed around and was entranced by the shimmer of gold Verarsoe's eyes shone in the light.

"The light shines your eyes to auburn," I whispered.

He smiled. "As yours are even in the dark. Sunlit hair and eyes like a darkened fire. You're beautiful, Victor."

I looked to my left, being sure there had been somebody standing right beside me. Thoughts found their way to my mind, but they were thoughts of blood and of evil, not the thoughts of mortals.

"There are…others here?"

"Yes. We are not the only ones."

It was as he said this when I noticed the gentle French accent breaking the English sounds into fragments.

He chuckled. "I hadn't remembered I had an accent."

I ignored his invasion of my mind and thought again about the others. The word came to me instantly, but it took me a long moment to say it. I said it quietly, not realizing he could still hear me.

"Satan's Own."

"I see Relone has told you things."

My eyes locked on him quickly at the surprise of his response to words I thought he hadn't heard, and he laughed quietly again like I had seen him do so many times before. He was strong and powerful, but something about him seemed tender, almost human. It was strange the way I felt. There was a kind of love I felt for him, and it seemed so unnatural that I should feel a love for him almost like the love I felt for my dead family. I didn't understand where such infatuation was coming from. I felt bewitched by every move he made, every word he spoke. He could stare solidly without faltering as if he were a statue. He aroused my curiosity and drew me deeper into the desire to understand. He fascinated me more than any story about him ever could, and I wanted him to keep me now.

He grasped my hand and led me off the bed to my feet. He sat upon a coffin and signaled me to the one opposite of him. He laughed when he saw the expression on my face.

"All right," he said. And we sat in chairs beside one another.

I started without hesitation. "What are we?"

"Vampires. Immortal."

"I mean—what are we? Evil? Mad?"

"Neither, I believe. Do you know goodness?"

"I don't know."

"Do you believe in God?"

"I don't know. Am I evil?"

"Do you want to be?"

"If I am, then what I want doesn't matter."

"You have a lot to learn, Victor. If you understand the concept of goodness and you obey by it, then you are good, are you not?"

"I can't say."

"Do you understand the word goodness?"

"Yes…I think I do."

"And evil?"

"I can't say. I've never really thought about it. What is evil?"

"You see?" He started smiling. "Does that question not make you good? Evil is only a point of view."

"I don't know."

"Maybe there is no evil that exists, but if there is—we are it."

"And that's…all right?"

"It's all right, Victor, to be what you are."

"But I don't know what I am."

"You don't need to be sure yet. Just do what feels right. Do what your soul tells you to do," he said kindly. "Vampires are said to be evil, damned, but they can possess mortal goodness and mortal passion as I see a lot of in you. Relone as well."

"As I see in you."

He shunned me in denial. "I am The King. I have no mortality left within me. You do. Immortal with a mortal heart."

"What about you? Are you evil?"

"I would say that, wouldn't you?"

"I don't know," I answered.

"And that is what we are."

"So, there are no answers?"

"Try again, Victor."

"I just want to know how to live, how to have a life."

"The way to exist, Victor Miller, is to contact your age, your era, your time."

"I don't want to change. I want to remain Victor Miller in 1745 and remember only what I care about."

"Then you will never have the answers you seek. You need to see through the surface of the world, Victor, and understand its soul."

"I think I can do that," I answered, nodding my head. "I do."

"So do I," he said softly, almost kindly—as my father would have.

"Do you want to hear the story that Relone didn't tell you?"

"I would guess that that's all I wanted in the first place," I answered, smiling.

He smiled too and let out a sigh before beginning.

About the Author

Sara J. Bernhardt is an author and poet who has been writing since a very young age and is a winner of several poetry and short story contests. It is clear that Bernhardt writes in a realistic tone while still creating the enthralling feeling of fantasy. Her writing puts readers in a world that they will truly love to be a part of. Though the writing is edgy and catching it is also not too complex which makes it a comfortable and enjoyable read for everyone.

You can follow Sara at these locations:
Facebook:
www.facebook.com/Sara-J-Bernhardt
Website: www.sjbernhardt.com

Other Works by Sara J. Bernhardt

https://books2read.com/HuntersTrilogySet

Summer's Deceit (Hunters Trilogy – Book 1): Jane Callahan is a reclusive, seventeen-year-old high school student dealing with the death of her beloved brother. Her home in Southern California with her mother is a constant reminder of her loss and pain. In hopes of escaping her past she moves to North Bend Oregon to live with her father, where she meets a beautiful boy named Aidan Summers. Jane is intrigued by his looks as well as his unusual ways of attempting to get her attention. After months of uncommon conversation and frustration, an uncertain romance brews between Jane and Aidan, but Aidan has a ghastly secret that could destroy everything.

Summer's Shadow (Hunters Trilogy – Book 2): Aidan Summers, a seventeen-year-old, stunningly beautiful genius, somehow finds his way into the life of Jane Callahan; a lovely girl trapped in soggy North Bend, Oregon. In this new

Tale by Sara J. Bernhardt, Aidan relates his side of the story. All of his dark secrets are revealed and all of his motivations behind his strange ways become known as the story unravels in a captivating narrative of suspense, romance, courage...and murder.

Summer's Redemption (Hunters Trilogy – Book 3): The secret alliance of The Silver Wing and the waging war with their evil rival, The Sevren, come into full view in a new light. The evil that still lurks and stirs behind the supposed destruction of The Sevren steps out of the shadows and spins a new tale of adventure, suspense, romance, mystery and terror.

In Gray

After a near fatal car crash brings Daisy Carmichael the ability to see the future, she is plagued by not only the things she sees, but the deadly secrets of the boy who saved her life.

https://books2read.com/InGray

Harvest Moon

Adeline Blackwood is a supernaturally gifted noble young woman who will do whatever is necessary to be with the man she loves.

https://books2read.com/HarvestMoonBernhardt

Also from the Lavish Family

A New Life Series
Samantha Jacobey
https://www.lavishpublishing.com/authors/samantha-jacobey/

Bikers, rockers and the FBI clash in a dark, mature adult romantic thriller – Tori Farrell will go through hell to get her new life in a completed seven book series!

To what lengths would you go to break away from a life filled with pain and suffering?

Tori Farrell has lived a dangerous life. When you grow up with a Motorcycle Gang of Mercenaries and Drug Lords like the Dragons, a normal life is more like a fairytale. For years, she accepted her dark reality, a world consisting of drugs, sex, violence and murder. In the end, she learned the most valuable lesson: survival.

After years of being ruled by the Dragons, Tori uses her skills of seduction and assassination to free herself from the grasp of the people who vowed they would never let her go. Taken in by the FBI, she fears not everything is what it seems, and soon finds herself lost in a web of lies and deceit. She thought getting away from the Dragons would put her on a path to a new and better life, but now she must face the cold hard truth... there is always a price to be paid.

Sinister Series
A. Nicky Hjort
https://www.lavishpublishing.com/authors/nicky-hjort-1/

Thrillers that will take you to the edge and leave you breathless! Mature adult reads due to graphic sexual and violent material…

Sinister Bouquet: Awakening - Book 1: Devyn Mitchell has a choice… listen to the voice of her unborn baby – or die- again.

After a near death experience, Doctor Devyn Mitchell finds herself not only mysteriously pregnant but able to communicate with her fetus.

She has two choices: give in to total madness or surrender to her new reality, which just may be the only way she and her family will survive the obsessions of the Homeless Hunter's mind.

A true paranormal romantic thriller, A Sinister Bouquet: Awakening, the first of the Sinister Series, will take you right to the edge of what you know to be possible and then drop you in a place so dark, so terrifying, that the only passageway out is through the blinding light of awakening.

Wake up.
Open your eyes.
Finally.
We've missed you so.

Sinister Vision: Know This Much Is True – Book 2: Elise Phillips, a doctor in training, has successfully repressed her kidnapping five years prior.

The only problem is...she has six and one half days to remember every terrible detail, or a total stranger will die. But to make matters even worse, in order to save this nameless woman, Elise will have to face something that scares her even more than death–intimacy.

Wake up. Open your eyes. Accept your assignment.
...The problem is not to find the answer–but to face it.

Know this much is true.

www.ingramcontent.com/pod-product-compliance
Lightning Source LLC
Chambersburg PA
CBHW072230190626
46809CB00017B/1681

* 9 7 8 1 9 4 4 9 8 5 9 7 4 *